DYSON

WALSH'S LAIR BOOK 3

KATHI S. BARTON

World Castle Publishing, LLC
Pensacola, Florida
Copyright © 2025 Kathi S. Barton
Hardback ISBN: 9798312573237
Paperback ISBN: 9798891263581
eBook ISBN: 9798891263598
First Edition World Castle Publishing, LLC, March 3, 2025
http://www.worldcastlepublishing.com

Licensing Notes

Cover: Cover Designs by Karen
Editor: Karen Fuller

Prologue

The Gathering Storm
~~The Peace of being without war~~
~~Evenness of mind, temper, and composure~~
~~Create by imagination, invention, and design~~

Storm walked around the little store listening to the gossip about one of the biggest disasters ever recorded — at least how these people were now witnessing it. She shook her head in amazement. How could humans be so insensitive? Not to mention stupid. That was one of the million and one reasons that she didn't hang out with humans for too long. They not only were, for the most part, clueless, but they seemed to have rose-colored glasses on all the time. The rumor mill was running full blast, it seemed today.

"They say that thousands of those bastards are dead. The whole place just split the roads and ate'em right up. Can't you just imagine what they were thinking when they were being swallowed up like that? I can't, I tell you what." The man behind the counter had himself a great audience, and he was taking full advantage of it today.

"Heard tell that them there houses just toppled over like the kid's blocks. Smashing people while they slept in their beds." The man speaking shook his head. "Mercy sakes alive. It sure did a nasty bit of business over there on that street."

"God is taking some sort of vengeance on them there foreigners. Sure as I'm a 'sitting here, it's God doing them people in." She actually had to physically close her own mouth when the person made that statement. "They should have stayed in their own place now here were we people are." Storm wondered if one of the people standing at the counter knew that they were all foreigners to this land.

She also wondered what they'd say about her and her sister if they knew what they really were made her smile. She wasn't going to speculate on it too much, but they'd have plenty to say. There was no doubt about that. They couldn't have gotten more foreigners than they were.

Storm and her twin sister, Ember, were time adjusters for the world. They, like a great many other beings, moved throughout time and made slight adjustments in the fabric of reality when and where it was needed, smoothing out the lines so that it looked untouched, perfect. They'd been doing it longer than any of the beings in this room had been alive. And they would continue to do so long after they were nothing more than dust in their graves. Humans and shifters alike had no idea how many times they'd been recused from their own stupidity.

To do their jobs, they would travel back and forth, sliding into whatever persona was needed to blend into the world they were in. It took great strength and lots of practice to even attempt what they did for the world. Sometimes, they were the only ones standing between the extinction of mankind and the world being populated at any given time. Storm caught a reflection of her face as she walked around the little odds and ends store.

Tall, at just over six feet, Storm was well-proportioned and athletic. Of course, no one would see that under her long dress and equally long sleeves. Her long dark hair, when not pulled into a tight bun at the back of her head as it was now, hung nearly to her waist in springy corkscrew ringlets. Her wings, too, pressed tightly against her back and legs only gave a small hint of what she really was.

Her skin, like her sisters, was alabaster and smooth as velvet. The only mark that marred their skin was the tattoo of their kind. It was a dragon that wore the wings that curled around their back and clawed hands, seemingly holding onto their shoulders while the tail trailed down their ribs and wrapped around their legs. Storms on her left leg, Embers to her right.

When their wings were spread and covering their arms from shoulders to their wrists, it would be, she supposed, frightening to anyone who would see her without any knowledge of what she was. Smiling at the men when they tipped their hats at her, she put her purchases on the counter and waited her turn to be waited on.

At the moment, Storm was in the year nineteen hundred and twenty-three in the body of a school teacher about to start "schooling" the area children in their reading, writing, and arithmetic. It was the closest body that fit her size when she popped into the time zone. The teacher would have no memories of her being Storm for a bit. There would be a slight accident, a small tumble that would alter her memories. Not that she'd remember Storm and what she had done, but the teacher would recover easily and never be the wiser of what she'd done for her world.

This time, working in this area, it had been a small fix. A mountain had come down on a family that was digging for clay and killed the youngest child. Storm had been tasked to save the child. Her future and that of a great many generations beyond her hadn't been born if she'd been killed. Saving the family, simply making them later than they had planned to the mountain side, had done the trick. The mom, always so organized, would forget to bring the cold water she'd stored in the creek that ran by their home to keep it nice and chilled for them all. Storm loved it when it was something like this had been.

There were times when whole realities had to be altered. Generations needed to be moved ahead to save someone. Sometimes, it was to save a being or one of the descendants of a human who was needed in the future. Other times, it was to erase a horrific time in the lives of humans — mostly, it was natural disasters where many deaths occurred. Humans, for the most part, would change up their entire lives, nothing to do with the ones that had been killed because they were witnesses to something so horrific that they had seen. It was all in the timing, she knew.

Other times it was the consequences of the disaster that were too large and affected too many things when they rippled down through the ages and had to be removed. Something as simple as a house being crushed with their things inside. It could have been the witnessing of a family pet being killed. Any and all things that would alter everything, and it was up to them to repair the damage that had been done.

As Time Displacement Officers, they were there to ensure that the shifts were smooth no overlapping lines after the time frame was removed or fixed. Storm would watch an event, something that she'd fixed a thousand times to make sure that things were normal. However, gifted humans or small children saw the flaws. It was easily explained as déjà vu. Or a dream, too. Small children would complain to their mothers or fathers about how they'd done this before, only to be told that they were wrong. Poor little tykes. She would believe her children, should she ever find one, she knew that.

Storm was also there to capture another of their kind and bring him to justice. It was he who had moved the family to the mountain for the one to be killed. And he would have profited off of the disaster had she not been there when it unfolded. That neither was something that they could let happen. Everything you did, even from pulling a leaf off of a tree, would affect generations of families, she'd come to learn. And that was the very thing that the other being was doing.

His name was Grail. He had been altering reality to suit his own personal gain and to profit for a while now, but no one could catch him. She was determined to find and make him pay before he could cause any more trouble. Altering a timeline too often would lead to sloppy work and time twitches that people would notice. And that was something that she was afraid of more than anything that she'd encountered in the human world. Too many glitches would wake the residents of the world to question what was going on, and it would — nearly all the time make them question their sanity.

Profit and notoriety from their jobs, both of which were laws that carried the sentence of death if broken, was what he had been doing today. Storm shuddered at the thought of the death he would endure when they took him back to Chilast, their magical realm. Death would not come easily or quickly for one like Grail. He had to know that. So why was he doing this when he knew it was only a matter of time before he was caught?

They didn't have the people to chase after him and keep the world and its people safe. As it was now, they were stretched to the limit. Working from sun up to sun down and all the between time too, it had been so long since she'd had a day off that she wanted to just lie down, pull some leaves over her, and get to sleep for about a thousand years.

Storm's twin sister, Ember, had gone to Tokyo to study and gather names of their kind for the continuation of their race. So far, all she'd been able to find was the list of dead. All of the dragons that had come after her and a few others who had been killed were on that list. That wasn't doing any of them a bit of good, and they all knew it. They were aging out, the lot of them and there wasn't anything that they could do about it.

It didn't bother their kind when they would wind time backward. It was the moving of time forward that would harm them. Time, it would add, even if it was only a click of a second to their age. And having to look at something over and over, forward and back, it might well add as many as ten minutes onto their long lives. After a while and all those adding up, a dragon would age quicker, worn down by time and effort, because without rest and some time off, they'd just fade away like all the other creatures in the world.

Storm had been sent to the Americas for her assignment to find and collect Grail before he could act on his plan. If they didn't find him, and soon, all the work they'd kept up with would be useless. They'd all be dead, and there wasn't anything that could be done about it after that.

But she had a feeling this time was different. They knew his plan, what he had needed and who to make himself in a new body to get away. It was what they had needed, what they were counting on to bring him to heel and to make all their lives safer without him in their worlds.

There was supposed to be a natural disaster, a large-scale shift in the earth's interior make up that would cause the entire state of California to drift into the deep ocean and sink, killing all the inhabitants there. There were people there that he needed to complete the next phase of his power play against his own kind. She had been sent there to make sure that it didn't happen and to bring Grail to the Laws of the Realm.

Those people, men, and women alike, were the pioneers of the future that Grail was manipulating. Their collective knowledge would be passed down to their children and then on to the next generation. They were brilliant and would revolutionize the world with Grail's backing and help. And not in a good way that would only benefit themselves and no one else.

They, like Grail, were evil and only thought to gain untold riches and wealth from sources within the different timelines that he was supposed to care for. From future records, the Time Displacement Office – the TDO and the Elders of their kind, knew that he had taken this opportunity to steal them away along with all their equipment. In the aftermath of the devastating slide, everyone would assume they had been killed as well. After decades of exhaustive tracing and retracing the lines of time back, the TDO knew this was where he made his first move to bring his plan to fruition.

But the quake, the distraction as it was never to happen. At least not where it had happened in the history they had studied. It had happened the day before in Tokyo, where Ember was studying and gathering information. She worried for her, and when she couldn't contact her, she just knew the worse had happened.

Storm had been trying to contact her sister for hours without luck. They were both immortals and could shift and fly away if danger was imminent, but with the suddenness of the quake in Tokyo and the horrific scale on which it had occurred, Storm feared her sister needed her and needed her now.

Storm felt the first touches of Ember as she exited the store. The feelings got stronger the more Storm concentrated on her sister's touch to her mind. It was all she could do to keep an eye out as to where she was going and thinking about her sister at the same time.

"Are you all right? I've been trying to reach you for hours. What's happened?" Storm said as soon as the link was snapped into place between them. Ember told her that she was fine, never better. "I've been so worried about you that I can barely breathe."

"There are signs of him here. I have contacted several of our kind in the area, and they say that he stayed with them for one night two days ago. I can smell him and his poison here deep within the belly of the mountains where the records are kept." Storm smiled at her greeting. Ember was never one to mince words when it came to their jobs.

"Did he hurt any of them? Ask them for their

help?" It would be just like him to murder them all just to throw them off his scent. But, at least for now, he only killed when he could gain from it.

"No. He spoke to no one but the people who were kind enough to allow him to rest at their dwellings. They say that he had a satchel with him, but he didn't seem to want to let anyone know what was in it. The Elders found a small thread, or we may not have known that he was even here. He's either getting better at hiding from us, or we're getting worse at our job, Storm."

"It's the same story here. He spent a night with the others here and then left. No one mentioned a satchel, though. He moved the place and altered the fabric where he had been. Ember, he didn't take the people he had before. Somehow, he has modified the events of that night yet again." Storm was suddenly terrified, and she was sure things were going to get worse before they caught up with him. "What do you suppose was in the sachet? I mean, is it important you think?"

"Moran, the one who was closest to him when he was here, said that it had photos in it. Some of them were old tin types, others digital, and one hologram. He thought they looked like me, but the eyes were the wrong color. I'm assuming that it must have been of you. Also, from what I could gather, there were images of the people in California. There…there was a picture of a man, as well. One that we've not encountered in all our searches as yet."

"Photos? Maybe he's using outside help trying to find these people. Makes sense that he would have pictures. He'd have to show them who to look for, right? No, he didn't take anyone as far as I can tell. It's…he's changed everything again."

There was a long pause, through their connection; Storm could feel her sister's tension.

"What is it? Something has happened. Tell me."

"The Elders, they called to me two days ago. They needed an extraction. I…they had me take a human away from a deadly shooting. I've no details yet, but he is to be guarded at all costs. I have him deep within the mountains with us. He is curious but not frightened. I think that is why there was a shift in the location of where the quake happened. I think we missed this man somehow, and we angered Grail by taking him. He was in one of the photos in Grail's collection. Storm, this man, he was to die."

"Who is he? Had he been taken by Grail before? Is he one of Grail's minions?" She was more worried for her sister's safety than ever before.

"No. He isn't like that. His mind and body are pure. His spirit is clear. The shooting I took him from killed the others like him – men who uphold the law.

I barely made it to him before the killings began in a house in New York. My wings were damaged slightly; I've been in a healing sleep until now." Still, Storm could feel her hesitation.

"Tell me the rest, Ember." She could have looked, she supposed, but in her current state, she knew that she'd hurt her sister. And she didn't want to do that. Hurting her would hurt her as well. "Ember?"

"I've been...the others here, we've...I've formed a bond with one. I've found my mate, Storm. After all this time, I've found my mate, and I'm afraid. Not of him, no, but what this is going to mean for the two of us. They will curtail my work soon."

Storm felt her heart stutter to a stop. Her mate, Ember, had found her mate. Storm moved to the outer wall of the store and leaned heavily against it. This would change everything. Ember could no longer help her with their job. As soon as Storm thought it, she felt horrible. Ember had found her mate. She should be rejoicing.

"Storm, please don't be mad. I didn't mean for this to happen." She had hurt her anyway. The tone of Ember's voice told her that.

"Don't be ridiculous. I'm happy for you. It's just a surprise, that's all. I wish you nothing but happiness and good fortune. I love you." Storm, stronger now because she had heard from Ember and knew that her sister was going to be all right, continued. "I'm going to contact the Elders and see what they want me to do now. You'll be all right for now? You're making sure that you're all safe while you work?"

"Yes, I am fine. Thank you, Sister. I will be waiting for you in our cave. You let me know when you will be arriving, and I'll be watching the sky for you."

Storm hoped it would be that easy, but knowing the Elders as she did, she doubted it very much. They would want something from her, and she'd do it because Storm was loyal to a fault.

~~Devotion to the continued existence of life~~

~~Devotion to the supreme good~~

~~Pure condition of body and mind~~

It was against the Laws of the Realm to appear before the Elders in any other form than the one that you had been born to. She didn't mind that so much as she loved being a dragon whenever she could. As soon as Storm arrived at the castle, she reached out to touch the magistrate to set up a meeting with the Elders and the Queen. She was both surprised and terrified that they had readily agreed to see her as soon as she had eaten and shifted.

Food was brought to her, and she enjoyed a large meal. As soon as she had finished, she knew that she needed to complete her mission and get back to her sister. Moving to the outdoor paddock just outside her suite of rooms, Storm began her shift.

She loved to be a human. Storm loved the soft textures of their skin, the feel of the hair upon the body. She also loved the way the fingers bent and was able to grasp things within them. The light feelings of simply walking would make her giddy with anticipation of stepping into the grass or sand with her bare feet. But to be her true self, there was nothing better.

Storm was a dragon, an Enneahedral Dragon — also known as a Ninefold Dragon. She was as rare as any being could be. Storm was the ninth daughter of nine daughters for nine generations. When she had been hatched, she had inherited all the elementals of the earth and the nine directives as well. Her powers were nine times that of her sister Ember — even though she'd only been seconds behind her in coming out of her shell and abilities that went beyond any other dragons.

With being the ninth in so many lines, Storm was to be Queen of their kind as soon as she found a mate worthy of her and her love. But she was in no hurry to find either. She was too busy to care for a lover and didn't want one slowing her down either.

As soon as she stepped into the magical arena, she let her body respond to the pull of her Dragon. First her body elongated, her spine curving and pulling, stretching to accommodate the large bulk of her form. Then her feet, dainty and small as a human, they too stretched and great claws formed at the toes. The wings at her back began pulling away from her body and forming into a great expanse, wide and full. Flapping them once, she felt the blood surge through them, and then she pulled them tight against her body. Her face molded and formed into a massive head, teeth a foot in length and sharp as the talons at her feet filled her mouth full and lethal. The human skin along her arms became scales of great strength, able to protect her from any weapon, small or large. Her scales shimmered in the moonlight, catching and reflecting the gold and silver that blazed within each protective shell. By the time the shift was complete, Storm was a massive twenty-five feet tall, seventy feet wide with her wingspan, and weighed several tons of pure muscle and bone. She moved to the large door that went directly into the throne room and bowed before the other dragons gathered there, careful of every step that she took.

"Mistress Storm, thank you for coming to see us so quickly. We have much to discuss." Storm dipped her head to hide her confusion. They had expected her?

"You must go to China. We need for you to bring back the man Alexander Walsh. It is imperative that he survives. He is vital to the future of our race, to all of us."

"Pardon me, Sire, but my sister, Ember, she is—" Storm started to tell them what she was sure that they already knew but they cut her off.

"Ember is going to have a hatchling soon. She must stay hidden. If Grail finds her, he will destroy her and the babe. No, it is you who needs to go and bring him back to us. May we count on you to serve us well, Mistress Storm?"

"Of course." Storm bowed before them and took a step back to leave the room. She was stopped by a slight cough from behind her.

"My lords, have you yet told the Mistress what is expected of her?" Storm startled. The being was small but in no means diminished in her stature. Standing before her was the strongest being any had ever known. Her mother, Queen of the Enneahedral Dragon clan, had swept into the room, her strength preceding her. "I will take it upon myself to do that now. You're dismissed." The people in the room disappeared at her command.

"Mother, you look well." Storm never knew how to speak to her mother, Morning. She had always intimidated her. Now was no different. Her beauty was one of the reasons, the other was that her mother wasn't really the affection sort of person. But then, neither was she.

"You look beautiful, child. I would like for you to shift and meet me in my private chamber. I should like to speak to you about this mission." Nodding once, her mother smiled. "We'll have a luncheon, you and I. And tea. I should like to speak to you about your other adventures, too, if you would allow it."

Immediately, Storm's body started its shift to human form. Within seconds, she was dressed similarly to her mother in a long silk robe with their crest blazing over their hearts. Storm nearly stepped back from her as Morning was standing very close. Surprisingly, Morning reached out and hugged her close to her.

The tightness of the hug had tears fill her eyes. It had been forever since her mother had hugged her, much less had hugged her first. Wrapping her arms around her mother, she heard her soft sob, and when she pulled away, her mother turned her back to her and started talking. As if nothing had happened.

"This man, Alex, you will bring him back to us safe. It's important." They were seated in the large room that her mother used when she came to the castle's offices. "I know that your sister is there, but she is breeding now. Thank the gods, and it's important to all of us that she be able to deliver her hatchling safely." Her mom sat down so Storm did the same in an equally ornate chair.

It was not a question, but Storm answered her anyway. "Yes. You can trust me to keep him safe."

"It's not his safety that I worry about. It's yours." Morning shifted on her seat. Her unease was evident on her face and posture. "Alex is your mate. It is determined by the Elders that he will father the next line. His bloodline is strong and pure. He will provide you with love and companionship for the rest of your life and on into the next. You and he and the family you breed will be the ones to destroy evil. "

Storm looked sharply at her mother. No. No, this could not be happening. She did not want a mate chosen for her. She stood and began pacing the room.

"You're angry. I don't blame you, I would be —"

"Pardon me, but you don't know me well enough to judge my anger. I will bring this man to you, but no one is choosing my mate." She turned on her mother, not sure that this was a smart move on her part, but she was pissed. "Was Ember's mate chosen for her as well? I'm sure that she'll be thrilled to know that her life has been arranged for her."

"No, her finding her mate was a surprise to us all. But this man, Alex, has been chosen as your mate since before he was born. And you will not use that tone with me, young lady. I am still your mother." Storm took a deep breath and then sat down when her mother asked her to.

"I miss said what he was to you, Storm. No one chose him for you. It was written in the tomes of the future. You will mate with him and bring children into this world that will be needed. When I said chosen, I meant that it has been written."

She stalked out of the room and into the courtyard again. This time, she shifted as she ran, her body forming and shaping as she went. By the time she had gone a hundred yards, she was launching herself into the sky and soaring across the night.

~~Enjoy great happiness~~
~~Maintain a fond hope for all kind~~
~~Uphold the reparation of magical energy requirements~~

Storm shifted to a human as she touched the ground. Her body threw off its form as if it were a heavy coat she no longer needed. She had landed close to the mouth of the cave where the man Alex was waiting.

Storm had contacted Ember when she left the Realm late last night. Telling her the events that had happened at the castle but she left out the part of "the man" being her mate. She did not plan on taking him as her mate, so she felt no reason to relay the news. Storm had also asked Ember to have the man waiting for her at the mouth of the cave. Storm did not want to take the time to go down and get him. The sooner she took him to the Elders and finished this assignment, the happier she would be.

"You're to come with me. I'm to take you to the Chilast," she said when she saw who she assumed was Alexander. She put out her hand to have him come with her.

"I don't think so. Not until someone explains to me what is going on. One minute, I'm on a domestic violence call. The next, I'm being wrapped in wings and brought here. Wings — I've seen some weird shit as a cop, but wings are something I've never encountered before." Alex sat hard onto the stone next to the wall. He looked stubborn and formidable. She was annoyed but impressed, too.

He was a very handsome man and taller than her by a good half a foot. His hair was dark, as dark as Storm's, but where hers was curly, his was straight and hung just past his shoulders. The shirt he had on had been torn, so she had a delicious view of his hard abs and harder chest. It looked smooth, and her fingers itched to touch, not just his chest but his entire body. Storm decided that she did not like him and would not be his mate, no matter what anyone said about it.

"I don't have time to explain, so get ready to go." She could feel the attraction to him and she hated him all the more for it.

Before he could say anything else, the earth shook beneath them. Alex fell to the cave floor, and

Storm was thrown to the wall, striking her head hard. While she fought the blackness trying to consume her, she threw a protective shell around Alex.

"Well, hello, Storm. You have something that belongs to me. I want him. Now!" Grail moved into the mouth opening of the cave, and Storm felt his power surge against the spell she had wrapped around Alex. It wouldn't work, of course; she was much stronger than him but it would weaken her more in protecting the human.

Grail had been a gray Dragon in color when Storm had first met him, his color bleeding into his human form, giving his eyes and hair the same rich colors. Now, he was black as pitch. His eyes, once a soft, rich, pewter color, were now black with his dark magic and evil. He was tall, as were all their kind, but he was also heavy. His lack of physical activity did not keep him in the shape he should have been. Though his face, dusky in pallor, was gaunt and shallow. She wondered how he could fly, much less take flight.

"You can't have him. I'm to take him back to the realm." She opened her magic and pushed hard back.

Grail raised his hands, and power appeared in the form of a ball of electricity. The longer he held it, the bigger it grew. If he hit the protection, he would destroy it. Storm needed to get them to safety now.

Storm moved in a flash to stand in front of

her assignment; she shifted partway, and her wings fluttered out from her back. She flapped them once and their powerful movement moved air strongly around the forest and knocked Grail to the ground as he stood in his fragile human form. Turning to Alex, she grabbed him up and ran to the lighted opening just beyond Grail. As she passed him, she felt a searing pain in her back but did not slow her pace. By the time she was in the open light, she was a full dragon, Alex tucked tightly in her talons. She soared high in the air just as Grail screamed at her to come back.

As a dragon, she could see all the areas where it would be safe for them to land. Her vision was perfect, and she could see the heat from any humans or animals below them, not wanting to land where anything could find them. Storm knew she was losing blood, but until she landed and got the man to safety, there was little to nothing she could do. She was getting weaker and knew that she would need to land soon or risk falling and crushing the man she was sent to protect.

Opening her mind, she hoped to be able to speak to the man. It was the way of their kind to be able to talk to their mates when there had been no bond at all between them. Unlike most species, she could have spoken to Alex since his birth had she known about him being what he was to her.

"Are you hurt? I should have asked sooner, but

I wanted to get you out of harm's way."

"No. I'm fine. Your claws are digging into me, but I fear that if you lessen your grip, I feel I'll fall to the earth — unless that is your plan? Tell me, Storm, do you plan to play toss the man into the air and see if you can catch him before he plummets to the earth. If so, could we not play today? I have a very busy schedule tomorrow, and if I'm crushed…well, it could put a crimp in things. No, I think a little pinching is preferable to death. I can smell your blood. How hurt are you?" She told him that she was, but she would heal when they landed. "If there is anything I can do to help you, please let me know. I'm pretty handy to have around."

She smiled at his sense of humor. Storm had not expected that. He was being very calm for a man who was being flown well above the clouds by a huge blue dragon.

"I must land soon to sleep and heal. I know of a place where you'll be safe until I can do both. No one will bother you there." She told him with as much reassurance as she could. Weakness was pulling hard at her, and she did not think she could go much longer.

"So you plan to leave me? I hope you don't expect me to sit around quietly waiting for your return. I may not know what is going on or why that other… what was he anyway?"

"He's a dragon like me. And you will stay where I tell you. You are to live at all costs. I don't have time to placate your feelings, human. I can easily say that you were eaten by Grail as not. Now be quiet." Storm began her descent.

Pain racked her body, and she knew that the landing was going to be hard. Seconds before she hit the earth, she dropped Alex and tumbled over him, careful not to land on him. As much as he irritated her, she did not want to kill him.

Her body shifted as soon as she stopped rolling, shifting to the last shape she had taken, hiding her true identity from anyone who would come upon her injured body. It was there to provide their kind with surreptitiousness.

Storm sat up just long enough to ensure that Alex was all right, her body and mind already pulling her to sleep. The area where she had taken them was hers; it was safe and hidden well from everyone, including any of her kind. She saw Alex stand and stride toward her just as blackness pulled her under.

~*~

Alex leaned over the woman he had carried into the house he had found a mile or so from where she had fallen. The fire he had lit in the deep fireplace reflected off her face, the reds and golds of the flames casting surreal shadows across her flawless cheeks. She was a beauty, just like her sister, Ember.

There was no doubt to him that the two women were sisters, as they were identical twins and as alike as any he had ever seen. He moved the dark hair away from her face and ran his fingers down her downy cheek. When she stirred slightly, he grinned. She was by far the most stubborn person he had ever met.

"Why do you look at me like that?" She looked up at him, her voice soft in the hushed room.

"I was thinking about how unlike your sister and you are. You are very beautiful, both of you. But you lack her softness and the…genteel nature that she has. You are strong and stubborn. And I've never wanted to kiss anyone more than I do you."

The expression on her face was priceless. He nearly laughed out loud but caught himself before it burst forth. He was afraid she would hurt him. Alex was not a stupid man; he had seen what she was, and while it was hard to believe, he was not going to dismiss the fact that she had flown them away from trouble.

"Why?" He asked her what she meant. "Why would you want to kiss me? It's not like I'm all that much. I'm, well, at least for the moment, just a woman who has the ability to change into a great dragon. Nothing special about that."

"Why would I want to kiss you, or why do I think

you're stubborn?" He touched her again. He could not seem to help himself. "And you are extremely special. I've only just thought of this too. You're extremely special to me for some reason. Do you know why?"

She looked at him for long moments, and he suddenly felt her touch his mind again, this time in a searching way, not to speak. Alex was not sure why he did not block her, but he would not try to fight her if she needed reassurance.

"You're a vampire. They didn't tell me that." She sat up on the side of the bed, but he didn't move back. It put them closer than before and he was happy with that.

"Yes, I'm a vampire. You're a dragon. I didn't know that you even existed until I met Ember. You say 'they'. Who? And who is that man who tried to kill us?"

"The Elders of our kind, they are the ones who sent me to bring you back to them. The other dragon, his name is Grail. He's also a dragon like me, a time shifter. Did Ember tell you what we do?" He nodded, and she continued. "He was there to kill you and me because we're supposed to be mates. We are to deliver the next line of dragons. Mother told me that our children were meant to destroy him and his reign. I didn't stick around long enough to hear why. Grail has been building his power base for many years and has been moving through time making adjustments in the fabric of lives to gather monies to fund his cause — to destroy all dragons but himself. I was in the Americas waiting for Grail to make a move to take a group of scientists away before they were to die, but he came here to get you instead. We had been tracking him for some time. The earthquake that happened in China was the result of him having a temper tantrum. Ember said that she had been sent to save you, but she didn't know why until I spoke to her. You see, you were to die in that last call you went on when on patrol. When Grail realized that you had survived, he unleashed his anger on those people."

"I'm sorry for them. I never meant to cause them harm." He was a good cop, and he never pulled his gun unless it was the only thing left for him to do.

Storm stood up and looked at him. The glow from the fire danced in her eyes. When she licked her lips, he watched, mesmerized by the pink tip moistening her lush lips. "Storm…"

Before he could claim her mouth, he felt himself being tossed across the room. Storm landed across his body, protecting him from falling debris. Her hand clamped tightly across his mouth when he started to speak.

"Grail." She said in a way of explanation. Moving quickly, she stood and pulled him close to her.

"I know you're in there, Storm, my dear. Come out and play with me, and bring our tasty friend along with you. We'll char him up and laugh over the silliness of all this fighting. I can offer you so much more than he could ever."

Alex pressed back against the far wall and flipped Storm around so that her back was now where his had been, and he moved hard to her body.

"As a human, is he as mortal. Will he die like a regular man?" Alex moved the thoughts through her mind. The words were fast and hard, urgent even.

"No. Yes. It needs to be silver through his heart, though. But his dragon would protect him by wrapping himself around Grail and taking him away. Grail would sense your movement, and as quick as you are, Grail is much faster. You can't...you can't think to beat him, do you? He'll take you, kill you."

"Do you care, Storm? Would you morn me if he kills me?" Now, his voice was a caress, a stroke along her heart and mind.

Without hesitation, without speaking in his mind, she answered. "Yes. Yes, I would."

"You are mine, understand?" He warned her. At her nod, he kissed her quickly and pulled his gun from his ankle holster. Winking at her, he took her hand and moved to the front of what had once been a small house.

"Please, Alex, please don't do this. He'll kill you." She whispered in his mind again.

"He'll try." When he started to step away, she pulled him back into the semi-darkness. "What?"

"You need to feed from me. I'll strengthen you, protect you. Feed from me, and my dragon will know you, and it'll keep you safe, keep us both safe."

Alex looked at her and smiled. He felt his fangs drop into place to feed. The need to sip from her nearly staggered him off his feet.

He wanted to savor her, make her his, and knew from her sister that dragon blood, especially Storm's blood was poison to those who did not ask and were given permission before drinking. But for those who had been allowed that rare sip, the benefits were amazing. Alex leaned into her throat, nuzzling her skin, tasting her with his mouth and tongue. Licking the area just over the pulse pounding in her neck, he pulled back slightly and stuck his bite deep and quick. Her moan ran along his skin like a caress.

At the first taste of her essence, he immediately felt the power surge into him. The more he drew from her, the stronger he felt his body getting. Alex was an older vampire, so his strength was not paltry, but with her surging through his veins, he felt extraordinary.

Pulling back reluctantly, he sealed the tiny wounds with is flick of his tongue. Moving his mouth along her jaw, he reached her mouth and sealed his over her heat.

"I know that you're in there, Storm. I demand that you come out now and face me. I have plans for us, plans that do not include that vampire mate of yours. Children of our union will bring me more money than I ever imagined."

Alex backed away from her slightly and saw the lust in her eyes. "If you stay right here, I'll take care of him, and we can get back to where we were before he interrupted us."

"I need to keep you safe. I need to stand at your side." He smiled at her possessive tone.

Moving and taking her hand once again, he hid his gun behind him as they walked forward.

"Ah, the future Queen and her stud. You know, I think I'm going to enjoy killing him. Oh yeah, this is going to be..."

He never finished. As he dropped to the ground, Grail stared at the smoking gun in Alex's hand.

Alex and Storm watched as Grail began to shift into several forms quickly before he just simply melted into the ground; his blue blood stained the ground beneath him.

There was a lot to be said for the element of surprise.

Chapter 1

"Hey Pops? Where are you?" Emma hadn't bothered knocking on the old man's front door since she was sixteen years old and had started living with him when things became too much at home. She followed the cursing that led her to the kitchen. "What's happened here?"

"That granddaughter." Emma knew just who he was talking about. Poppy, Pop's only grandchild, had been to see him. "She decided that I wasn't eating healthy enough. How the hell would she know? I've not seen her since Christmas, that was nearly eleven months ago, and she comes barging in here thinking to cook me...who uses flour to make oatmeal, I ask you. Or, for that matter, seventeen pots and bowls? No one, that's who. It's going to take me a week to get all this flour out of the walls and curtains. Someone should have beaten her more as a child."

"You don't mean that." He just glared at her. "Go sit down, and I'll finish your meal for you. Also, clean up. Why is there milk in the trash can?"

"She said that it was cow's milk. What the

hell does that mean? Where did she think that stuff comes from? Heaven?" She told him what she knew. "Almond milk? Christ love a duck, Emma. How the hell does one go about milking an almond? They don't have teets, do they? How would that even be a thing?"

"I don't know, but I'll have to get you some more groceries. She must have gone through all your cabinets and tossed things out. It looks like she poured out your coffee, too. I'll make a list." He was still grumbling about the teets on almonds when she put a large bowl of oatmeal in front of him. When he asked where the honey was, she only had to point to the trash can to know. "I'm going to bar her from coming here again if she can't keep her hands and thoughts about my eating habits to herself. I've been around for nearly a hundred years, by golly and I never heard of such a thing as eating healthy that didn't cause indigestion. I need my oats every day, or I don't poop. I have to poop, or I die. Don't she know that?"

"Pops, there are times that I wish I didn't know as much about you as I do. Now eat, and I'll clean up the kitchen. You didn't let her in the pantry, did you?" He said that he didn't think she knew that he had one. "More than likely not."

It took Emma an hour to set the kitchen to rights and make a good grocery list. He'd insist on going with her, and she didn't mind that, but he wasn't going to be driving one of the carts around. She was sure that ninety percent of the bruises she had last time she left there were from his driving. And he purposely liked to accidentally run into people still dressed in what he assumed were their night clothes.

He never spoke to her while she was driving. Fearful of her losing her concentration and killing him, his fear since his wife had been killed in an accident by a distracted driver, she had plenty of time to think about the relationship that she had with his family. It wasn't a good one, not even close, but she never stepped foot in the big house again after turning sixteen.

Emma had been born without a name. No first, and no sir name. Her mother, or father, she didn't know, had dropped her off at the firehouse when she'd been a newborn. Not even having her cord fall off, she was estimated to be only a few hours old. Then, she was sent to stay with a family that worked in some indirect way for the system.

After three months, she was taken to the Gregory household. From the very beginning, she'd not been welcome. She'd been taken in so that the wife, who had already had Poppy, could get pregnant. Their thinking was, and it turned out to be not true, that when you adopted a child, meaning her, then you'd finally get pregnant.

For sixteen long years, Mrs. Gregory, Poppy's

mother, and granddaughter to Pop, would tell her every week that she wasn't her daughter, but their plan was going to make sure she had another child. And as soon as she was with child — a term that she'd come to learn the hard way, Emma, what they had named her would go right back to the children's home and not be heard from again.

Every single week, she'd go to the doctor to be tested, and every week when she returned home, Emma would be punished — she didn't have all that much — by having her things taken from her, including supper for a week.

As soon as she was sixteen years old, long past the time that Mrs. Gregory could become with child, she was ordered to move in with Pop Marshall and his wife to become their servant. After that, she never stepped foot in the Gregory house again.

It, of course, never was like that between them. And before long, she'd been adopted by Pop and his wife so that she'd be able to have a last name, he'd told her. No one in the Gregory house knew about that. To them, she was still Emma, the girl who didn't belong.

"Whatcha thinking about, there, Emma? Some planning going on in that head of yours?" She told him that she was thinking of the things that she might need at her home while she was here. "I'm not paying for it. You know that, don't you? If'n I do, that daughter of mine will take away my ability to get around again."

"I know that, Pop. I have the money to pay for my things and yours if it comes to that." He said that he might have to owe her, as Poppy had taken the cash he had for her gasoline. "Figures. They have more money than sense, and they're stealing from the man who created their way of living."

After getting him set up in one of the electric carts with the promise of not hitting anything or anyone, they did their shopping. When she noticed him look longingly at something, like a new flavor of tea or some ice cream, she'd put it in her cart to give him when they got back to his place.

"How about when we get back to the house, we have us a nice cookout? The weather is gonna turn soon, and we might as well enjoy it while we can." She agreed with him and asked him what he wanted. "Can you do me that salmon that I love so much? The one with the rice with it? Oh, that's my favorite."

She ended up paying for the salmon as it was out of his budget the family had him on. He only gave in when she told him that she'd used the leftovers in her lunch for the following week. As soon as they were back at his home, she set him up to take his evening nap, put the groceries away that she'd gotten with his money, and started dinner.

The two of them had become best of friends

over the years. She literally didn't have anyone else and he pretended like he didn't either. The man had run a multibillion-dollar company for nearly all his life right from the ground up, and when he'd turned eighty-five, he was retired by his son-in-law, and his daughter put him on a very limited strict budget. He came into the kitchen just as she was setting up the table for the two of them.

"I got me an idea. I want you to tell me what you think about it. Now, don't be thinking with your heart, child, but your head." She told him that he owned all her heart, so she didn't know how that was going to work. "Ain't you the sweetest thing. All right. Then try to listen to me before you tell me no. I don't want to live here anymore." She was afraid that he meant to move into the house with his daughter and granddaughter, and she'd never be allowed to see him again.

"Where did you want to go? You know that I would follow you to the moon and back, don't you? You're my hero." He took her hand into his and held it to his face while he cried a little. "I'm sorry, Pop. I didn't mean to upset you."

"You didn't. I was just thinking hard about the fact that I don't have my blood family saying such things to me, and it broke my heart for a minute. But I won't be moving into that daughter of mine's house. And the big house, I lived there with my Sally, and I don't think I'd last a day being there again. Besides, I think they'd kill me off. No, I want to look into some nursing homes for me. The kind that lets you get out and about sometimes. It would be nice too if I could cook me some meals, you know I need oatmeal every day and they won't be tossing out my things because they don't like it. Will you help me out with that?"

"You know that I'd do anything for you. But they're not going to like that. I believe you've said this before, they enjoy having you here in this little apartment where they can keep an eye on you. They still don't know that I come here every day, do they?" He told her that he'd not want them to know, that he'd already fixed it up with his own attorney. "All right. Good job in getting ahead of them. When do you want to go? I'm assuming that you have a place all picked out."

"Yes. I do at that. I'm going to stay at the Little Bit of Sunshine home, the one next to your place." She said they'd have a fit. "Honey, they don't know that you're still around, much less helping me out daily. I can't imagine what they think was supposed to happen to me with them leaving me all by my lonesome. Not even once a month do they come here and bother with me. Unless they need something from me. And we both know that they're not needing any advice from an old man like me."

"Are we leaving in the darkness of the night? Packing you up and leaving like you've not paid the rent or something." He laughed, just as she hoped that he would. "When do you want this to happen?"

"Tomorrow. I've been sending things out by my attorney for the last couple of weeks. You've no idea how terrified I've been thinking that you'd tell me that I'm better off here. With this move, I can see you every day without you having to travel here. I can go to your house too. I asked. You'd be my second in command if anything should need to be talked about. I mean my death, so's you know."

"I don't want to talk about that part, but yes, I know." They'd made a promise, the two of them. When it came time for either of them to die, they would go on with life as if nothing had happened. Like that was ever going to happen, she thought. But they had promised.

As she was piling his clothing in the back of the rented van, she thought of all the things that could go wrong with this. He could fall, break a hip, and she'd be in trouble again. But he was happy with this move, happier than he'd been in a while, and she was going to do it for him if it was the last thing he ever asked of her. Damn it, he deserved so much better than he had right now.

~*~

Sidney didn't know what was going on with the family, but he wasn't going to be suckered into anything right now. Not that they'd make him be a part of something when he didn't want to, but he had things going on, a purchase that he'd been waiting for since he'd been a young hatchling. With this buy, he was going to be able to expand things in the south end area just the way that he wanted it. No more malls. Not only that, but he was going to be putting small one and two-bedroom apartments that would be furnished for the homeless. He'd been without a home once when he'd been out on his own for a while, and it hadn't been anything that he wanted to happen to anyone. Not even some stranger that he met on the street.

His brothers Madison and Dyson joined him. "Hey, did you want to get some dinner with me? Layla is…what's the matter with you? You look like you've been caught at having girly magazines in your room, and it was Dad that caught you." He told his brother Dyson what he was doing. "I would have helped you with that. You know that Layla would have been on board, too."

"Everyone would have taken over. They still, even you, think of me as the baby, and that—" Dyson pointed out that he was the baby. "I know that. I just want something of my own to work on. I have the money and the knowledge of what needs to be done.

Stay out of — " Dyson took a deep breath and let it out slowly when he saw the look on his brother's face.

"All right now. Do you want to start over with that? I mean, I'm not mad. I still have my bouts of anger, too. But I was just asking you a simple question." He told him he was sorry and that he knew that. "But? What's going on?"

"Nothing and everything. I feel like I'm sneaking around in the dark doing this, like when I skipped school that one time. Remember that? I was sick for a week because I'd done it. Come to find out, I didn't skip at all because the school had been closed down due to the weather. Christ, I'm such a dork sometimes." Madison told him that he was a dork all the time. "Thanks. I knew that I could depend on you to real things out for me."

The three of them hugged then Sidney pulled out the planning sheets for his idea. After explaining a few things and answering a couple more questions, he could tell that Madison was finding fault. He asked him what he'd found wrong.

"No, I'm not. Just let me absorb, will you? You're worse than Kyle when it comes to letting people help you out." Madison looked over the plans again. He did ask some questions, good ones that he'd not thought of as he went through the blueprints, too. When he was finished with it, he told him that he liked it. "I don't know that I'd make them furnished. That would be difficult to make everyone happy even if you gave them golden beds or something like that. But I would go ahead and do what you said about the kitchens. Having them a part of the walls would make it less likely that stuff would be stolen. But it's a good, solid plan, Sid. You should be proud of yourself."

After making notes on the things that both Madison Dyson had said, he and his brothers went to dinner. Layla, Madison's mate, was out doing things with their mom, so she'd be out for a while. Sidney loved his new sisters-in-law, but he was terrified of them both, including his mom, too. But then he thought that everyone should have been terrified of their mom.

Madison leaned back in his chair and spoke to Dyson and Sidney. "Did I tell you about the dragons on us?" Sidney had told him that he'd only heard that they had them but not if they had any special meaning. "I didn't either, so I asked Grandma. Mom wasn't sure of all the details, so she had me go to her. Did you know that Mom is terrified of her mom? I didn't know that. Bares some thinking on, I believe. Anyway, they're there to protect us as humans. Even our mates. The reason that Fowler didn't get one is because he is now living in the other world with Mom. But when he's here, he'll have one on his body as well. I think that's fantastic. However, it's the talking part that I need to get used to with her."

Sidney laughed. "Her? You have a female dragon on your back? Cool Beans. So I guess that means that Layla has a male one." He said that they balanced each other. "I guess I can see that. What does it feel like when they move around? I think I meant to ask that of you before, but I forgot."

"It's kind of creepy if you ask me. Layla thinks it's like a warm blanket being pulled up and over her. I can understand that feeling, but I'm used to shifting and having a warm blanket, so to speak. But, as I said, she talks to me." Sidney laughed, asking him if she would talk to him about his sex with Layla. "I knew you'd ask me that. But no, she doesn't bother me in the bedroom. However, and this is the really strange part, she talks to Layla's dragon. And this is wonderful. If she's in real danger, like a house fire or flooding, I'm not sure what the circumstances might be, but he can lift her up and carry her to safety. We've not seen that yet, I don't know that I ever want to be in a situation where she's in that much danger, but it's wonderful to know that she can be safe." Sidney and Dyson both agreed.

"Will we all get them?" Madison told him that they would. "What if we find a dragon as our mate? I mean, that's still possible, right?"

"I will have to ask about that. I didn't think of…

do you really think that's possible? To find a dragon mate?" Sidney didn't know, but it was something to think about. "At any given time, there are dragons around us. I don't know how many, but I would say a few. Hiding in plain sight as we've been doing for centuries. Mom and Aunt Ember would know, too. They have the most power of all the others around. Even grandma."

"It's scary to think of the power that Mom has. I know that Dad has a great deal with him being an old vampire, but when I think of the length of time that Mom and Aunt Ember have been around, it boggles the mind." Madison and Dyson both agreed just as their food was being brought to the three of them.

It was steak night at the restaurant. All you could eat night. They would come here to get a couple of their really wonderful steaks but never eat their fill. The place would have to shut down afterward if even one of them got enough to fill their dragon.

"Remember when we were younger, when there were fewer people around? How we'd fly the skies like we owned them? I miss those days a great deal." Sidney told Dyson that he didn't remember that period of time, he might have been too young. "Yeah, I guess so. But I do. We were so revered, too. Families would raise cattle just for us to come and eat."

Sidney loved hearing about the stories from

when they were younger. He didn't have as many, of course, things were different when he came along, and they had to be hidden away. He did remember a time that was special to him and told his older brothers about it.

"There were unicorns around when I was a hatchling. Mom would set me in a field and let them watch over me so that I'd not get into trouble. She would work, checking on me occasionally, but they were more mischievous than I was then. They would steal whole pies from the kitchen and bring them out to share with me. Or entire gardens of flowers would be eaten by them." Madison said that Mom probably knew, and Dyson agreed. "Yeah, Dad, too. He would come and get me before Mom would and get me cleaned up. I remember thinking at the time that I'd gotten away with something so grand. Those were the good times."

"You miss that? I don't. I know that you were never around when Grail was but he was terrifying. And then there was Great-Grandma. I don't think that you had as much to do with her as we did, what with her being forced to retire. Some of the things that I could tell you would—"

"Tell me, Madison. Please when you think of something, tell me. I don't want to sound whiney, but being the youngest, I missed a lot with that. I'm not saying that I'm jealous of the things that you guys had to go through. I know from Dad it was scary, but I would like to know about it. Please?" Madison told him that he would, that they all would get together sometimes and talk about the olden days. "Thanks. I know that some of it is painful for you guys. Like it still hurts Grandma to think about losing her mate. I don't know that I could have taken it as well as she did."

"She didn't lose her mate, Sidney. He faded." Sidney said he was sure that someone told him he was no longer around. "No, he's not. He decided right after Grandma took over the realm that he wasn't needed, so he faded into a garden. No one talks about it, of course. He wasn't…you'll have to have Grandma tell you. He wasn't thrilled about being second best to Grandma. I mean, he wasn't a mean person, and he didn't cause any trouble but he didn't care for when someone came to the castle to talk business, he was asked to leave. I might well have, too, but he was very jealous of the magic that they had."

"I didn't know that. See? This is why we have to talk about this stuff. I didn't know that my grandfather, not that I'd go and look him up, but that he was still around ready to shoot the shit with me." They both laughed and when they were finished with dinner, the three of them walked around the town. It really wasn't much of a town here. But it did have about the best steak house he'd ever been to. "I'm going to have to look up the owner of this place. I bet I could talk them into having one closer to where we live. They have the best salmon filets that I've ever had."

"And their desserts are perfection. I'm going to have to bring Dad back here when he's ready. He loves all things lemon, and their lemon blueberry bread is the best that has ever been…now I want some." They turned and headed back to the place when the lights went off. "Well damn it. Now, that's all I can think about. I'll have to come buy some for Layla tomorrow. I'll make a list if you want me to pick some things up for you."

He did give his brother a list. All he could think about now was their crunchy loaves of bread. It was the best with soup. Sidney could eat an entire dozen of them while barely touching whatever else he was having for a meal. Laughing, they made their way home, talking about how they would come back here for all major decisions as it was the best place to do that in.

Driving home, Sidney thought of himself having a mate. He really didn't mind finding her. He'd seen enough of the mistakes that his older brothers had made that he felt like he was going to be the perfect mate for her when she came along. At least, that's what he kept telling himself.

Pulling into his driveway, he thought of his grandma. He missed her and decided that he was going to go and visit her right then. Gathering up the magic that would be needed to take him to her, he was so happy that she seemed to be expecting him. After several hugs and her telling him how welcome he was, they settled down in the garden to enjoy each other's company. It was her, oddly enough, that brought up her mate.

"He has missed so much since he'd gone away. I think about him often, but I don't want him to come to me just because I get lonely at times. With Fowler and Amy here all the time, the pain of being alone is lessened a great deal. And when one of you boys comes here like this, it will make my entire week in just being around you. What do you have going on? Tell me everything."

He told her about the housing development that he was working on, and she agreed with what Madison and Dyson had said about the furniture. She told him that they'd not take care of it very well if they didn't have to work for it. He agreed with her and said that he would make the changes in his plans. When she cried a little, he went to her and hugged her, asking her what he'd done.

"Nothing. Not at all. It's just been a long time since I've had someone to agree with me and not do it because I'm their queen. Or I was at one time." He told her that he thought that everyone still thought of her as the queen. "Thank you, Sidney. You've no idea how much that means to me."

After talking well into the next morning, he decided to stay there in one of the rooms that was reserved for him. It was wonderful to be able to just relax and talk to someone without thought as to whether or not they were agreeing with him simply because he was a dragon. Or the grandson of the former queen.

"Your lordship? There is a phone call for you. It is very important, or I'd not have awakened you." Sidney sat up and looked around, unsure of where he was for several minutes. "Sir, it's a woman by the name of Emma Marshall. She said that you were acquainted with her from school."

"Yes. Yes. Just give me a second here." Wiping his face with his hand, he tried to remember how long it had been since he'd seen Emma, much less heard from her. Taking the phone, an odd-looking thing that he'd never used before, he said hello. "Emma, is everything all right?"

"I've been arrested." He could hear both anger and her being upset in her voice. "I don't know who else to call, Sidney. I have the money to bail me out, but they won't allow me to get into my house to get my cards. I'll pay you...I just realized how late it is. Listen,

I'll call you tomorrow if I can't work something—"

"No, I'm awake, and I'm very happy that you called me. I'll be there...do you still live in Trinway?" She told him that she did and that she was sorry to have woke him up. "Honey, it's just fine. I promise you. I'll be there in about half an hour. I hope everything is all right. Is it?"

She burst into tears, and he was wide awake then. Letting her talk, trying to make out what she was saying, he willed himself to his own home. While he had no idea what she was saying, he knew that it was serious. As he made his way out to his car, he finally got her to talk to him.

"They said that I tried to kill my grandfather. I'd never do that. He's all I have in the world." He told her that he knew that, too. "He's in the hospital, and they won't let me see him. Then, while I was trying to get in, I was arrested for attempted murder. I'd rather die myself than harm him. I think they're just pissed off because he moved out of the house and into a nursing home where they can't get to him."

He didn't know what that meant either, as she was babbling again. When she told him that her time was up with talking to him, he told her that he was leaving his place. It was the longest twenty-minute drive he'd ever driven.

When he got to the station house, since he knew

nearly everyone there, Sidney was taken back to see Emma. She was a mess and it looked like someone had taken a few pops to her face. While she cried, not really saying anything, he was able to hold her. Her trembling body told him what her words didn't. She was very upset.

"His daughter is Mrs. Darling Gregory. You remember me talking about her, right?" He knew the story, and it pissed him off every time he heard her name. "Well, she told the police that I hit her. Then, I held Pops in front of me while she tried to defend herself. Which is in no way true. I would never let him take a blow for me. But she hit me like she did when I was younger."

Once she was put into a room where he could talk to her, he got more of the information from her. When he paid her bail, a great deal more than he thought it should have been for having the shit beat out of her, Sidney took her to the hospital. She was going to need stitches if he didn't miss his bet, and he wanted her to see if she had a concussion.

Calling his dad when he needed help with the hospital, he was glad that he'd brought Mom with him. There was some major shit going down here, and he, for one, was glad that his parents weren't the pushover type. As soon as he introduced them to Emma, Mom seemed to take her under her wing and guided her to not just the emergency room but also got someone to see her right away.

"The power of love." He asked her if she loved him or the drama. "The drama, of course. And I do like this girl. She's upset now, but I bet she has a fire under her."

"I don't know that I'd call it fire, but she has been mistreated all her life. Even from infancy. We met in high school." He told his mom what had happened to Emma when she'd been born, with Emma interjecting in places something that she would remember. By the time the film had been read about her, she did indeed have a concussion. She was given a room, and food set up for her and Mom not leaving her side.

It was more than he could have hoped for. Going down the long hall to the elevators, he made his way to see Pops Marshall. He loved the old man like he did Emma and was sorry that the elderly man had gone through so much. As soon as he saw him, Pops begged him for information about his darling, and Sidney was glad to be able to give it to him. It was going to be a very long night, but he didn't really care. They were both safe.

Chapter 2

Emitte Marshall, better known as Pops, watched the nurses go in and out of the room. He'd been back at the nursing home, Little Bit of Sunshine, for a week now and he was finally figuring out the way things were supposed to be going. He thought that getting the lay of the land, so to speak, was the only way he was going to fit into the place. And he liked it.

"Mr. Marshall, did you get yourself any lunch yet?" He said that his granddaughter and adopted daughter, Emma, was coming to eat with him. "Oh, how nice. Is she doing all right now, too? I heard that she had to spend a couple of days in the hospital after the last time you were here."

"Yes. Got herself a concussion. She's doing better now that my daughter and other granddaughter have to stay away from the two of us." He'd nipped that in the bud right fast. He'd called his attorney when he'd gotten out of the hospital, pressed charges against his family, got control back of all his money, and then bought Little Bit so that he could change the rules to suit himself. They weren't going to be bothering them again, by doggies. "She'll be in here soon enough, I'm thinking."

There she was, coming through the door like she was supposed to. Glancing at the clock over her head he was thrilled that she knew how much he hated when people couldn't show up on time for meetings and the like. She was two minutes early. And durned if she didn't bring that friend of hers, Sidney Walsh.

"I bought you some company, Pops." She was the only one who called him that. His family thought that it was just too undignified for a grown man to be called Pop like he was a soft drink or something. "Sidney has been brushing up on his chess, too, so that you can have someone else to beat. And I brought hamburgers too. I know you love them."

They didn't talk while they were eating. He was all right with the quiet, too. It gave him the worst kind of heartburn when someone wanted him to think while he ate. So he appreciated Emma telling Sidney the same rules. After they were finished up, Emma cleaned up the mess and he and Sidney got down to some serious chess moves.

"I heard from your attorney, Mr. Marshall. He said to tell you that everything is just the way that you want it to be here and with Emma. You're back to full control of everything." He was glad that Sidney was discrete about what he said and spoke when Emma was out of the room. "He also said to tell you that the big house is going to be cleaned from top to bottom. Were you going to sell it off?"

"No, I've not decided just yet. Emma said she can't afford the place what with the furnace bills being in the triple digits. She don't know that I left everything to her yet. She'll be able to afford it without any trouble then." Sidney nodded and moved his rook. "I say there, you don't love Emma enough to marry her, do you? It would do my heart a bit of good to see her married off and someone to take care of her. My family, they ain't gonna like her getting everything when I pass on. No sir. They're going to be fit to be tied."

"No, sir. She's not my mate. I have other brothers, three of them that haven't met her yet but that might be a bust too. Melbourne, Edgar, and Dyson aren't mated yet, but they're very set in their ways. I'm the only one that is a free spirit." They both laughed. Emmitte thought that the young man was charming and smart and told him so. "Thank you, sir. I appreciate that coming from you." The game was forgotten when the young man told him of his family and what they were.

"I knew that you and that family of yours had been around a good long time but I had no idea that you were dragons too. I would imagine that your parents are ancient, too." He told him how his dad was a vampire and his mom a dragon. And that all six of his brothers were dragons with some vampire traits. "Good to know. Wouldn't it be good to have our Emma hooked up with a dragon? They'd surely protect her better than I can, that's for sure. I worry for her, you know. Once I'm gone, they'll take everything out on her. My wife Sally, rest her soul, raised her as our own, even going so far as to adopt her so she'd have our last name. Darling, my daughter, she didn't want a thing to do with her other than to adopt her, thinking that she'd get in the family way so she could take her back to the system that they got her from."

"That's sad. I know that it hurt Emma when she told me about it. My heart broke for her when she was just a kid." He asked him how long he'd known his Emma. "Oh, about ten years. I knew her from high school, and she was hanging around the college campus when I was going there. I don't think that she actually took any classes then but sat through them so that when she could afford it, she could do better in the classes. She did well from what I'm to understand when she finally got to go."

"Yes, sir, she did better than all right. Got her self graduating at the top of her class she did. Smart as she can be, too." Emmitte moved his piece only to have it captured. "I guess she was right in telling me that you were good at chess. How about another game?"

"I'd love that." Emma joined them a few minutes later with a grocery list in her hand. The girl was forever taking good care of him, and when she said she'd be back, it was hard for him to let her go out alone. One of them durn kids of his would get at her, and they might not stop at giving her a terrible headache. "She'll be all right, Mr. Marshall. I've sent a faerie with her. He'll keep her safe from any harm and he has an entire pip to—" He had him explain what a pip was. "Oh, a group of faeries. They'll keep her safe from any and all harm. I promise you that they might be small, but they're very dangerous when they need to be."

They were just finishing up their third game when Emma came back. She was happy, her face just bright with smiles. After telling him that she'd gotten him some ice cream, they all shared a dish of the treat, and then it was time for them to go home. Sidney told him before he left that he'd run her by his brothers on the off chance that she was their mate. After they left, Emitte went to the sunroom to take a little nap. He was glad for the new games that had been provided with his purchasing of the home, as well as a few more televisions in the place.

Startling awake, he took a few minutes to figure out where he was and what was going on. There was a little bit of a fuss about what to watch on television, but he didn't think that it was going to amount to much. Getting up, making sure that his cane was close by, he made his way to his room to catch up on some of the things that Sidney had brought him to look over.

Unlike most of the older people in Little Bit, he knew how to make a computer work for him. He could look things up and get into his email account without any trouble. All thanks to Emma.

She'd been good for him and Sally when she'd been living with them. She was smart, articulate, and had a good heart. He could sit and talk to her for hours on end and not be bored. And as far as his multibillion-dollar businesses, she knew a lot about them, too. He'd taught her everything that he'd known, and she'd been brilliant at it. She was going to fit right in when he passed on and he couldn't have been happier about leaving his money and businesses to anyone but her.

Pulling out some of the things that she'd gotten him at the store, he had him a large bowl of soup beans. It wasn't as good as his Sally's, but it was a good enough substitute. After dinner was over in the dining room, he made his way there to watch a little TV. He had one in his room, but he liked to watch Jeopardy with some of the others around him. He'd been watching it in the big room since he'd been here.

At bedtime, around nine o'clock, he was set up to sleep until the breakfast bell rang. He'd have his bath finished up and dressed for the day by the time his bowl of oatmeal was on the table. It was nice being able to eat what he wanted, too. He was nearly one hundred years old and he thought that if he'd made it that far, people should leave him alone about what he should and shouldn't be eating. His durned granddaughter wanted him to eat healthy. He told her to blow it out of her butt.

Darling had never been a good daughter. Emitte blamed it on her husband, Wally. He'd spoiled her good when they were first married, and she now expected everyone to do the same for her. Thinking that she needed her butt beat a little more, Emitte thought that she'd do well to beat her daughter too. Poppy. What sort of name was that for a kid, he wanted to know.

Just as he was turning off his lights, his cell phone rang. The only people who had the number were Emma, Sidney, and his attorney. Answering it with a little caution, he was happy to hear from Sidney. The first thing he asked him was if he called too late.

"No. I was headed to bed, but I always have time to talk to you. What's going on?" He told him how Emma was going to have dinner with his family tomorrow night, and he wanted to know if he would like to come too. "My goodness. Yes, I'd love that. I hear that your mom can put on a good feed bag. I'll be happy to…someone will have to come and get me. I don't drive anymore. Reflects are a little slower than I want them to be."

"I'll pick you up when I get Emma. She's not real keen on coming over, I guess she's still not used to being around a lot of people but she's coming because I told her that I'd ask you to come." He asked him what he would have done if he couldn't make it. "I was going to talk you into it because all my brothers will be there. I thought that way you can see for yourself whether she's a mate or not. I don't believe that she is, to be honest. I've been talking about her for a decade, and they all feel like they know her already. But it will be a good dinner. Steaks and baked potatoes. Also a nice green salad like you like."

"And some of that crusty bread that Emma tells me that your momma makes. That's something that I've been—you don't have to put your momma out, young man, but if she has an inkling to bake some bread too, I won't turn that down either." Laughing, he said that he'd ask her. "Good. Don't you be telling her to make it for me. I'm not going to turn down a good meal and not be invited back again on account of me wanting something she didn't want to make."

"My mom only does what she wants even if someone was to beg her for it. She's a wonderful person and I'm slightly afraid of her. I'm sure she'll not have any trouble making sure that you have a good

loaf of bread that you can take home with you, too."
They both laughed, and it made him feel good. "I'll
pick you up around five o'clock. That way, we can talk
a bit before dinner."

He was a bit too excited to go to bed but he made
himself get into the mood to sleep. To be having dinner
with the family was something that he never expected
but he was looking forward to it as much as he had
anything in his life. Kissing his Sally's picture, he told
her about his day and how much he loved her. He was
on the fence about going to see her soon. He thought
that she'd be mad at him if he left too soon. Oh, but he
missed her something terrible.

~*~

It was just a little past five when he pulled up in front
of the nursing home. Emitte was just where he said
he'd be. Waiting on the front porch so that they'd not
have to get out of the car. Emma had to get out to hug
her grandda, and it brought tears to his eyes to see how
happy the two of them were to see each other. When
he knew for a fact that they'd seen each other just this
morning and had a lunch date, too.

"My mom said to tell you that she's going to
bake you bread once a week so that you have a nice
treat." That made Emitte a little teary-eyed, but he
thanked him for it all the same. "She has some jelly
and other things for you to take back with you when

you leave. She said that she has plenty now that we all don't live at home anymore, so you're welcome to it."

Letting the older man gather his emotions, he changed the subject to what he and Emma had been talking about before they'd picked up Emitte. He told him that since he was a might older than him he should just call him by his first name. Sidney was honored to do that for the man and thought that they could be very good friends from now on.

"I'm bringing you to my house for two reasons." Emma asked him if it was her stellar conversation. "Something like that. But my brothers are going to be here, and I wanted to see if you were mated to one of them. It's all good if you're not, but I'd love to have you as part of my family."

"I'm not your mate, am I?" He shook his head and looked at her when he stopped at a light. "What if I am? What's going to happen then?"

"To be honest, the only thing that I know for sure is that you're going to be taken care of for the rest of your life. And that you'll never have to worry about your family getting the better of you. Also, my brother, if one of them is your mate, you'll be loved like no one has ever loved you before."

"I have that with you and my grandda." He told her that it would be different. A long and lasting romance, too. "I don't know about that, Sidney. I don't have my life together enough now to hold down a job, much less have some guy that I barely know to want things of me that I don't have in me to give to him."

"It won't be like that. I swear." He hoped he was right but right now, he didn't know. He's seen how his brothers had been to their mates. He worried, too, that the saying that mates couldn't hurt one another might not apply to Emma. She was pretty mean when she wanted to be. "I've told you so much about them over the years that I'm sure that you could pick them out on your own. And since Fowler and Madison have their mates, they have changed a great deal in their mannerisms, too."

"I don't know. I feel like…I don't know what I feel. I'm worried that I'll be a huge disappointment to whoever wants to marry me." She looked at him. He could feel her sadness as he drove the last few blocks to his parents' home. "I'm not much of a girl that you guys would want to be around. I mean, even my own parents didn't want me and dropped me off at the fire station when I was only a few hours old."

"It doesn't matter if you are or not one of their mates. You still have me in your heart, and I have you in my life, and that's more than I could have hoped for. I love you, Emma. I will for the rest of my days, too." She turned away, and he allowed her the few minutes he drove so that she could compose herself.

As he pulled into the driveway, he thought about his brothers and didn't know if he wanted one of them to be her mate or not. They were very stuck in their own ways, and Emma was a free spirit. He loved that about her, too.

Mom and Dad met them at the door. He was never so proud of them as he was in that moment. They were welcoming his friends into their home and he loved them for that. As hugs were given, Mom looked at him and winked. He had a feeling that not only did Mom know who Emma was mated to but that she was already immortal like they were, as well as her grandda. Christ, he so loved his family.

Each of his brothers stood up when they entered the living room. It was a rare treat to have both his parents here. They'd been staying in the other world with Fowler and Amy for the last few weeks. It was great to have them all together again.

After introductions, it was Dyson who kept standing when the others had settled down on the couches. He was wondering what was wrong with him when he simply stared at Emma. Dad popped him in the back of the head, and he finally sat down. Emma asked him if she was his mate.

"Yes, I belong to you." She rolled her eyes, and that seemed to tickle his brother in some way. "While I'm not sure of things right now, I'm going to make it my life work to make sure that you're going to live a long and happy life."

"What makes you think that I'm not happy with my life now?" Emitte put his hand on Emma's leg, and she apologized to Dyson. "I'm sorry. I'm out of sorts because my family is trying to make sure that grandda and I never see each other again. I can't handle that. He's the only person that has ever believed in me."

"I believe in you. And while I don't have a home, when I find one the two of you can live there together for as long as you wish. No one will ever harm either of you, nor will they be able to get into the house with ill-will in their hearts and minds."

"I know about you, Dyson. A little, anyway. Sidney used to talk about you all when we were hanging out together. He's been my friend and confidant since I was just a kid." He told her that he was glad that she had someone in her corner. "Thank you for that. I don't know what I would have done if you were to have told me that I couldn't see him anymore."

"To do that would mean that I'd not see him either. And I love my brothers, my entire family too much to not be able to see them anymore. Much like it is with your grandda." Dyson grinned at him. "Thank you for keeping her safe, Sidney. I owe you a great deal."

"My pleasure." Dinner was called, and the

family went to the dining room. It was wonderful to be able to call Emma and Emitte family. He also wasn't as worried about the two of them as he had been before. Life was suddenly taking on a new outlook. And he couldn't have been happier with the way things had turned out. He hoped it would just get better and better, too.

Chapter 3

Emma wasn't sure what to think about being a mate. For some reason, it seemed like she'd been set up in coming here tonight. Not really set up, but blindsided with her having a mate and all that would come with that. Grandda was talking to Dyson about things, and she found herself on the couch talking to Morning, Sidney's grandmother. She came to dinner tonight, too, so that she could meet her.

"I'm not really someone that knows how to be mated to a very wealthy man. I'm sort of like one of those people behind the scenes." Morning told her that she'd do just fine and that she was happy that Dyson had someone in his life, too. "He looks sort of stressed out. Is that because of me?"

"I think Dyson is stressed out a great deal. He's a good man and, of late, has been working on projects with Sidney. They're putting together things for the homeless. I'm going to be helping with that as well." She told her how she was homeless for a while until her grandda took her in to be their servant. "That didn't work out the way that his daughter wanted. He took one look at me and decided that I needed a last name. So he and Grandma Sally adopted me when I was just barely sixteen. I've been thrilled since so long as his family isn't around."

"I'm to understand that they don't like him being in the nursing home. Nor that you visit him so much." She explained to her that they don't like her at all and that they want to keep Emitte close so that he doesn't go spending what they consider their money. "Greedy bastards, I guess."

"You have no idea. They wanted to cremate Grandma Sally when she passed because they thought it would be cheaper. They told Grandda that it was stupid to spend money on a dead person when no one could care. Turns out that nearly four thousand people came to pay their respects to the couple, and that burned their asses big time when Grandda had to pay for extra calling hours." She laughed with Morning. "You sound like bells when you laugh. It's very nice."

"I'm glad that you told me that. It's been a long time since I've been able to get out and about. My daughter Storm and her husband Alex have taken over for me in the magical realm. They're doing a wonderful job, the two of them, and I couldn't be prouder of them. Alex is such a wonderful mate to my daughter. Even Ember, Storm's sister, loves him like a brother."

"That's nice to hear. I've never heard all that

much about Ember. Sidney talks about her but it's usually in conjunction with other family members. I'm to understand that she has four children of her own with grandchildren." She smiled so big that it felt like sunshine on her. After telling her their names, she was shown pictures of them. This was a wonderful grandmother like Grandma Sally had been.

They talked about magic, and while she was sure that she didn't have any of her own, Morning assured her that she had some. It had been from Storm and everyone else that she'd hugged since arriving.

"Your grandda is going to be all right as well." She asked her what she meant. "Well, he's your family which makes him a part of ours. He'll live a good deal longer should he wish, and he'll not have any of the aches and pains that a man his age would have. He'll be like he's in his fifties again. But he doesn't have to take the immortality. He'll still be in good health, but he will die when it's his time. If that's what he wants."

"I don't know what he'd want. He's sort of set in his ways a bit." Morning said that they all were. "Yes, I can imagine when you've been around as long as you guys have, you do get stuck with things longer." Again, they both laughed. And she was feeling more relaxed around the woman. Sidney had told her that his grandmother could snuff you out with just a point of her finger if she was pissed off enough. Emma didn't know if he was serious or not, but she was going to be on her best behavior from now on. Even Storm didn't scare her as much as her mother did.

Dinner was fantastic. They had steaks and chicken from the grill, baked potatoes, green beans, and a hardy salad too. Grandda ate nearly a whole loaf of the crusty bread that he'd asked for and was nearly unable to finish his steak. By the time that dessert came, they were all groaning about how full they were, but it didn't stop them from having some pie and ice cream.

"I was just telling Dyson here about my house." She nodded, so exhausted all of a sudden from the carbs that they'd eaten that she didn't speak. "I told him that since I'm going to be leaving it to you that I'd just as soon the two of you move into it now, and that would save the two of you from having to go out and look for something together. It's a fine old house, you know that, child."

"It is a nice…what do you mean you're leaving it to me? I'm not your daughter." He told her that the state of Ohio thought that she was. "All right. You did adopt me, but your daughter is expecting to get that house." He just smiled before speaking.

"I know she is, child. And I'm assuming that right now, she's picking out curtains for her bedroom. But I've given her enough over the years. She and her deadbeat husband forcing me into retirement and only allowed me a small pittance to live on with my own money by declaring me incompetent, and all the money that she's taken from me and her mother. All the times that I had to bail her out. These are things that I've kept track of since she was sixteen years old and totaled two cars before she even had her licenses. Besides, I don't have to give her anything. But I should mention her in my will. Simply because I want her to realize that it wasn't a mistake that I didn't give her anything. Well, I did leave her something. A bill for all the things that she took from me when her mom was alive. That'll get her goat."

She loved to hear her grandda laugh. Especially when he did it with his whole body. When he started to slap his knee, his lack of control over his humor made her laugh, too. She loved this old man more than she could have ever explained to anyone.

They talked about the house and what it had in it in ways of rooms. There were eleven bedrooms, counting the master suite. Six bathrooms on the second floor where the bedrooms were and two on the main floor. There was, of course, one in the master suite that took up the entire third floor of the house. There was an extra room there that had been built as a nursery with a maid's room, but all it had been used for was for storage for holiday décor.

The kitchen had a large pantry that held enough

groceries for a month in it. A walk-in freezer that also held enough meat in it that would tie them over until the next month of food. There was an eat-in kitchen in the large room as well as a pretty little place that was near the back door and the windows there so that a couple of people could have tea there. Or a light breakfast.

She loved the dining room. They didn't use it all that much when she'd been living there, but it still had fond memories of the times that they did. It was an oval-shaped room with windows that looked out over the expansive backyard, almost within touching distance. The table that was in here wasn't as large as it would pull out to be. With all the leaves in the oak dining table, it would serve sixteen people. Around the room, there was a scattering of chairs that went with it when necessary. The rest had been stored in the pantry where they were easy to get to when a large group was expected to dine with them.

There was a library that held a large office desk that her grandma used. She said that she loved the smells from the room—mostly the old book smell mixed with fresh flowers that would fill the room when in season.

The four-corner fireplace only needed to be lit in one of the downstairs main rooms and it would be seen in each of the corner rooms. The living room, dining room, library, and sitting room. That had always been her favorite feature in the house to have a single fireplace for all the rooms that one could roam to.

The pool house was about ten yards from the house. The pool, one that was heated year-round, was in the ground and deep enough to dive in. The kids from the neighborhood used to come and play in the pool with her in the summer but Darling put a stop to that when she started to charge them for the privilege to use the thing. That had pissed Grandma Sally up so badly that she didn't open the pool for even family after that. Telling Darling that if she thought she could make the rules, then she would show her who the boss really was. It had been an ongoing fight since she had passed away, and grandda simply kept up with the tradition just to keep Darling and Poppy from coming over and taking things from the house.

Marshall Manor sat in the middle of fifty acres that surrounded the house. There were about two hundred more acres that were used to supply things for the household in the summer months, but for the past few years, about twelve, she thought grandda had been renting the land out to farmers so that they could have a little more in their barns come winter. She thought it worked out well, and if she really was going to own it, she would keep things the way that they were simply because she didn't care to put in that much gardening right away and have to have more help making it last through the winter months. She'd have to ask Dyson what he wanted to do.

They made plans to go over the house in the morning. She'd not be able to be there, she told them, as she had three appointments in the morning to make sure that her job was still for her. Darling and her husband Matt had made it so she wasn't able to go to work for the three days that she spent in the hospital when they'd beaten the crap out of her over grandda moving into the nursing home.

"How do you suppose she's going to feel when I move back into my home with you and Dyson?" She told grandda that she thought that if Darling could get to him, she'd be fine with that. He was shaking his head. "Dyson told me that there is enough magic in the family that they could make it so that no one with ill will could enter the home. Not even if they were on the outside shooting into the house will anyone be harmed. I think I like that bit of magic. What do you think about it?"

"Do you think it'll work because she's family?" Grandda said that he said it would. "Well, I'm all for no one being able to get into the house to hurt any of us. How far extending does it go? I mean, will it cover the yard too? I'd just as soon she wouldn't be able to even do that, wouldn't you, Grandda?"

"I'd surely love to be able to sit out on the deck out back and not have to worry about any old fool trying to kill me off. I might even have the pool opened if it was to cover anyone coming over to have a good time with it." She said that she'd like that as well come summer. "We'll talk to him. Did Dyson tell you that he's going to wait until you can go with him to see the house? Nice young man, that boy. I know that he's a mite more older than me than he looks but I see him as a boy nonetheless."

Taking Grandda back to the nursing home, he was dozing on the way. She hated to wake him up to go inside, but he was all right with that. He'd had a wonderful time and had so enjoyed the company that he wanted to do it again. But not put anyone out. She loved this old man more than she could have anyone else in her life, and he told her that he loved her as well.

Dyson took her to the place she'd been renting for the last few years. It wasn't much. She had three rooms and a bathroom that was all hers. There was parking for her car, but since it seldom ran, she didn't think much about it. She used to be within walking distance of the grocery store, but it burned down a few years ago, and no one replaced it. There was a Dollar General in town, but she didn't do her grocery shopping there like most of the people living in the complex with her did. Usually, she'd just hitch a ride with someone who was going there and come back with them.

"This isn't a good neighborhood here. I'm sure you know that." She said that she doesn't spend much time here, only to sleep. She'd been working two jobs since she started working, and it was all right for her. "If we do move into your grandda's home, your home, I guess, will you still need to work that much?"

"I still need to keep up with my bills. I don't have a great deal, but I've been supporting myself for a few years now, and I don't care for the feeling of not having some money in the bank to keep me from being homeless again. That's something that I never want to have to do again." He explained that what he had was now hers, and what she had was hers as well. "You can't have enough money for you to give it all to me. That would be just stupid."

"I'm wealthy, so in turn, we're both wealthy. If you wanted to give a million dollars to every man, woman, and child in this town, we'd still have billions of dollars left over." She told him that wasn't possible. "However, it is true. I've been around for a very long time, and in that time, I've been able to invest in things that have become very profitable. Also, the saying about dragon's tears is true. I have banked all of those, too and have quite a bit of gems and jewelry that is just laying about to sell off if I were to ever find myself short of funds. In all my years, that's never happened."

"And only knowing me for the short time that you have, you're willing to give it over to me as if you've not been saving all your life." He said that it would be his pleasure to give it all to her should it make her feel like she was safe and secure. "I don't know what to think about that. I mean, even saying you have one million dollars is a lot for me to think about. But to have that much, in the billions, is more than my mind can comprehend."

"However, it's all true." He put the car in drive, and the two of them left the area. "Is there anything there that you have to have? Any kind of family things that you need tonight?"

"There is nothing in the place at all that can't be replaced. I have nothing but a few items that I even paid full price for." She looked at him as he pulled up in front of one of the nicer shops in town. "What are we here for?"

"We're going to get you what you might need for the next couple of days—shampoo that you need, toothbrush. Things like that. Then I'm going to take you to a hotel where I know you'll be safe." She asked him why. "There isn't any safeguard at that place like there will be at the hotel. No one will know you there so the other family won't come looking for you. Once we move into the Manor, if we do, then I know that the magic there will keep you from being harmed. I worry about you."

She nodded and got out of the car with him. While Emma didn't know what he thought she could afford here, she was willing to see what they had. The little boutique was full of the prettiest things that she'd ever seen. And she wanted it all.

~*~

Never had he done any shopping with a woman and getting things for her. Dyson found that he was having a good time. At first, she was looking at things that she wanted but could afford. Then, after he picked out a nice dress that he thought would look good on her, he found other things that he wanted to see her in. By the time they were being rung up, she had enough clothing to last her a couple of months. He didn't care. It was fun being able to afford whatever she wanted.

"I don't know what came over me in shopping like this. I was going to blame it all on you, but I had a wonderful time as well." Dyson agreed that he had as well. "Good. We can't do that all the time, but I can't tell you that it wasn't a blast."

"I enjoyed it as well. It's the first time in my life where I didn't look at prices when I wanted something. I mean, I really didn't have to do that at all, but I certainly enjoyed the look on your face when I found something that I thought you'd look good in."

she smiled at him, and in that moment, he thought that he could go for the rest of his life on the feelings that it had given him. A simple smile from a mate did that for him. "My mom got in touch with me while we were there. She wants to know if she can go over to the house and make it safe. I told her that I had hoped to have it done soon and she wants to make sure that everyone that lives there is as safe as she can make them. She's already gone to the nursing home to take care of that. She told me too that three employees weren't able to enter the place when their shift came up." Emma asked them what she'd done. "Figured out that they were harming the patients that were bedridden and some of the ones that were confined to wheelchairs in order to get around."

"That's terrible." He agreed with her just as they were pulling up in front of the hotel. "I'll have to let your mom into the Manor, won't I? Or can she just slip in without anyone being the wiser?"

"Mom won't need to get into the house right away. But in order to make it so that your grandda can sit on his porch and enjoy himself, she'll make the land surrounding the place a safe zone for all of us living there. I'm ready to move in now. I figured that if you liked the house, I will as well. And your grandda had done such a wonderful job describing it to me that I think I could find my way around all on my own."

"He loves that old house. He and my grandma lived in it from the time they were married until she passed away. After they forced him into retirement and declared him incompetent, they forced him to move into a small apartment where they could keep an eye on him to control him. When he moved himself into the nursing home, one of the others would bring him back after beating the shit out of him. They liked him living where no one was watching over him so that they could get to his money and other things in the house." Dyson told her that he thought that was sad, too. "It is. Darling and her daughter lived there for a while, right after I was forced to move out, but since there wasn't any kind of internet around the house, they couldn't stand it. I'm going to have to figure out a way to get at least cable for him. He's enjoyed watching the old westerns on television as well as some old shows that he and grandma watched when she'd been alive."

"I'm sure that one of the faeries will be glad to do that for him. They enjoy his stories, and he treats them well when they show themselves. I think that a couple of them would live out their days with the elderly man just to be able to say that they'd been around someone so great. Your grandda is a good man." Emma said that she thought so as well. "I like him. He says what he thinks, and that's a wonderful thing."

"When my grandma was alive, she used to scold

him when he was so vocal. Then, toward the end of her life, a few years, she became just as blunt. I remember once when they'd gone out to eat, Grandma hadn't liked her fish dish. After sending it back to be redone, they simply gave her the same fish on a different plate. She was fit to be tied. Not only did she demand to talk to the chef on duty, but she had the entire management team trying to make things right. And you know what they did? Left a huge tip because they knew that it wasn't the waitstaff's fault but that of the cook. I don't believe they stayed in business much after that. A bad review from them would make a lot of people stand up and take notice. They felt bad about the closing, putting all those people out of work, so they made sure that those who wanted one had a job at one of their factories. I believe a great many of them still work there."

After getting a room for each of them, he went to his room after carrying up a bag of things that Emma would need tonight. It occurred to him that she could change at will if she wanted to, but he thought that would have been less fun than shopping. He might have to do that more often, shop with her just to see her eyes shine in happiness.

Going to bed after hearing from his mom. She was going to meet with them tomorrow evening. The staff had been made aware of them coming there for dinner, and the house was being cleaned from top to bottom tonight and into tomorrow. He was glad for the extra hands. While he'd never been in the house before, Emitte had assured him that there were rooms that had been closed off in a while and they would need a good cleaning. He was looking forward to touring what he was going to consider their forever home. He only hoped he wasn't putting too much faith in what Emitte had told him instead of what was really going on with the house.

Chapter 4

Darling wasn't at all happy. And when she wasn't happy, things didn't bode well for those around her. She looked at her daughter, Poppy, and told her to get her feet off the table. She moved them, more than likely sensing her mood, but she'd wanted to fight, and her doing what she asked wasn't giving her what she wanted.

"When I find that girl, I'm going to have her cremated alive." Poppy didn't say anything, which was good, she supposed, but it did make her more pissy. "Don't you have anything to say? I'm needing an outlet, and you're not giving it to me."

"I know. I'm still nursing bruises from the last time you wanted to fight." Darling huffed. "Where is Father? Shouldn't he be here taking some of your anger? I don't like to be the only one that's around to feel the pain, Mother. And what are you so hyped up about anyway? When the old buzzard dies, we'll have it all."

"I don't know anymore." Poppy asked her what she meant. "Well, he's terribly cozy with that girl,

Emma. And she's stuck so far up his ass that I'm sure that she'd telling him things about us. True or not, she should just keep her mouth shut."

Darling had hated the child since she'd been brought to their home to make it so that she'd have another baby. The old saying that if you adopted a child, then you'd get pregnant wasn't as true as people thought. For sixteen whole years, she'd put up with that brat only to never have another child but Poppy. When she'd been told that she was too old to carry a child, she'd shipped Emma off to her parent's house for her to be a slave for them. Little did she know that they'd take the child as their own, going so far as to adopt her as their own child. Darling supposed that made her a part of the family, her step-sister, but she didn't care to share anything with her, so she never acknowledged her in any way. She looked at her daughter.

"They told me from the start that you were supposed to be a boy. All eight months that I carried you, the scans came back that you were a little boy. How I so wish you would have been one sometimes." She told her mom that she was glad that she was a girl. "Of course you would. Because you don't know how things work in the financial world. My father would have left it all to you had you been a boy and not given Emma a second look. But since he didn't have a grandson to hand things over to, it's going to take me some time to get your father to turn the running of the company over to me. As the rightful owner."

"I don't know that Grandfather thinks that way. And why would he turn it over to Father? I don't think that he even likes him all that much." That was true. Her dad hated David more than she did at times. Of course, he was lazy as fuck and drank too much, but he had stayed with her even after having numerous affairs. Even those hadn't produced another baby. "Do you think that he'll live much longer? I mean, isn't there some kind of rule that states that after a certain age, they have to be put away? I think that's a good rule if you ask me."

"No, that's not a rule. Even though I like that too, they'll let people in their hundreds run around and rule the world like they have some kind of experience or something. Father should have died some time ago, like when Mother died. Had he done what I wanted and been in the car with her, then none of this would be an issue. They'd both be dead, and I'd be spending all his money like I should be able to do." She thought about killing her mother off, and it pissed her off every time she thought of how Dad hadn't gone with her to the meeting that she went to every Wednesday night. Damn it all to hell and back. "I think his funeral arrangements are all settled like mom's were. Had I been in charge of them, I would have had her cremated and no service. But that fucking funeral director thought that people would want to come and see him and wish him a good life. I wonder if he realized that he was spending my money? Stupid bastard. And there is no way to kill him off, either. The man is a nuisance, and I wish him and his family would just die, too."

Darling had heard somewhere that the director was a vampire. That he sucked the blood from the dead, and that was what kept him alive. She also heard, too, that vampires couldn't drink from the dead. While not knowing what to believe, she'd tried to get into the funeral home to test the theory, and he'd been waiting for her. Since then, she didn't go to anyone's funeral for fear of the big man. Christ, what was this world coming to when you couldn't even trust anyone to be human anymore. Stupid bastards, all of them.

"Mother, did you know that someone said that the Walsh family is considered to be the richest people in the world? I think that it was in the newspaper last month. We should try and get into their good graces somehow." She asked her if she thought that was true. "I don't know why not. Have you seen the houses that they all live in? They wear designer clothing even when walking in town. Could be that they're richer than grandfather too."

"I doubt that. He's a millionaire several times over. There aren't that many people around here that have as much money as he does. Even if they say they do, who are you going to believe." She thought of something. "Are any of them single? I mean, you might be onto something by saying something about getting into the family. What would you say to marrying one of them? Or at the least pretending to be knocked up by one of them so they have to take care of you."

"I have no desire to have any children. For any reason. I'd rather be homeless than to have some baby sucking the life out of me." She shivered, and Darling asked her what experience she had with children. "Minx has three of them. They cling to her like she's a tree and they're a bunch of monkeys. Christ, when one of them isn't sucking at her tit, the other two are sitting around in shitty diapers screaming to be changed. No way, no how am I going to even pretend to have a kid for money."

"All right then, that's a good thing. No grandchildren. And if dumbass gets with child someday, it won't be related to me only by adoption. Why they did that is beyond me. She was supposed to be their servant, not their child. I don't need a step-sister for Christ's sake." She decided to look up the Walsh family on her phone. "Christ, Poppy, they are more wealthy than Father is. It says here that their wealth is uncalculatable there is so much. I think that I could count very far, and they're saying it's more than that."

She read how two of the brothers were married and that they were a happy family. Good to the community as well as anyone that needed help. They talked about some of the investments that they worked on as well as how they were responsible for the pool in the city being open all the time as well as some of the charities around town able to be so generous with their funding to help out the homeless as well as others that were around. They were a big deal. Perhaps she'd find them out and about and try to sink her claws into one of them. It was worth a shot, she told herself.

The front doorbell rang, and Poppy went to answer it. After calling her to the front door, she had to sign for a registered letter that was from a law firm of Shuttle and Shuttle. Not bothering with thanking the man, she closed the door in his face after he told her that he had recorded her receiving the letter. The man had some nerve laughing at her when she asked him what it was about.

Opening the letter up, several business cards fell to the floor. While having Poppy pick them up, she read the letter that had come with them. Sitting down hard, she was shocked to see that her father had gone to all the trouble of letting her know that he was moving into the big house again with her step-sister Emma Walsh and her new husband.

"It says here that I'm not allowed on the property, nor am I going to be able to set foot in the house. What the fuck does that mean? It was my childhood home." She didn't bother trying to figure out what Poppy was saying but continued to read the letter. "It also says that while I'm mentioned in the will of my father, I'm not going to be receiving anything but a bill of laden for all the things that I'm supposed to have stolen or borrowed from him and never returned. What the hell kind of bullshit is this? I don't owe him anything? Emma put him up to this. I just know it."

"Does that mean that I won't get anything either? Not as his only grandchild?" She told her that there was no mention of her. "Good. Maybe that means that he's going to be leaving it all to me. That would be wonderful. Now you have to be nice to me, or I won't allow you to live in the big house with me."

"You'll have me living there, or I'll kill you where you stand if you try anything like that." She just looked at her, and Darling went back to the letter. "Oh, here it is. It says that any offspring that I've had will not be considered family either and that they will not be mentioned in the will. I suppose that means you since you're the only offspring I've ever had." She was on the second page when she had to put the letter down.

"What is it, Mother? Did he say what he's going to be doing with his money? If he leaves it to some charity, I'm going to be really pissed off. I've been waiting my whole life for some of that cash, and he'd better not be giving it away to some down and trodden place that doesn't need it as much as I do." Darling didn't say anything to her daughter, thinking about what the rest of the letter said. "If you're not going to tell me, at least let me read it. I don't like the look on your face, Mother. I need to know."

"He's giving it all to Emma. Every stock and bond, every piece of property. Home and car. All of it is going to Emma as she has been his rock since she'd been his child." She thought of the last line of the letter. "He said that he's letting us know so that we can move on with our lives and not think about ways to get back at him or Emma since it would result in us being put in jail until well after he's gone. It's as if he's thinking that now that we know, we'll just give up on the money and the house and act as if it's all right for him to be turning it all over to her. Christ, I'm going to be sick."

She laid back on the couch she was on and closed her eyes. However, it was as if every word of what he'd said to her was burned into her brain. How could he do that to her? This wasn't right. None of it was.

"What are you going to do?" She couldn't think past the thought of what her father, her only father, was doing to her. "Mother? What do you want to do now? You're not going to just give up, are you? That's not like you at all."

"I need to think, and I can't do that with you jabbering all the time." Poppy was pissed off and huffing and puffing all around the room. "Poppy. For Christ's sake, will you just shut the fuck up and allow me to think for a minute. The entire world had just taken a big dump on me, and I need to figure out what I'm going to do about it." Poppy took the letter from her fingers and looked it over. "You're not getting anything either. That's not right either. It mentions your father, too, on how he's not even mentioned in the will as he doesn't like him either."

There were other things that had been said in the letter. How she was to pay back the four point three million dollars that she had borrowed from him over the years. The other two million dollars in things that she'd taken from the home and sold. It went on to list those items as well as the money that she'd gotten for them. How did he know that? How did he have such an exact price on the things that she'd taken to sell off and where she'd sold them too.

She must have fallen asleep at some point and woke up to an empty room. Good. With Poppy gone, she'd be able to think better. She did love her daughter but there were times that she wished she'd never had her. All she did was run her mouth on things that didn't concern her and go on about things too that she had no idea what was going on. She needed to talk to her husband. Maybe he had an idea of what they could do to get their money back from her father.

"I got a letter from him as well. Right here during a business meeting." Darling told him that Poppy had been here with her. "Yes, it does mention that any offspring that you had wouldn't be getting anything either. I wish I had an attorney like his. Whoever it is, they're good. Not a single loophole that I can find. And I looked hard, too. Did you read the business cards that came with the letter? He's been tested for being sound of mind, so you can't even get him on that either. Also, he has a clean bill of health from his doctor. There isn't even a loop that we can use saying that he's not fit to be making changes like this to his will. Christ, Darling, he's going to do it. Take away all the shit that we've had to put up with over the years. Had I known he was going to do this, I swear I'd of never married you in the first place. Much less had a daughter. What plans do you have now? I think he's well and truly fucked us over. So anything you come up with will have to be solid."

"I don't know what to do. Killing him off won't do me a bit of good. The will has been changed and filed. He made it a point to tell me that as well." David said that he'd seen that too. "Poppy is more than likely going to go and try to suck up with him to see if she could get into the will as well, but I don't see that happening. It's too little too late, I think."

"Poppy never cared for him or the manor. What does she think she's going to say to him that will have him change his mind? That she's had a change of heart? He won't believe that any more than I would." Someone spoke to him, and he answered. "I have to go, Darling. Now that things aren't going to go our way, I'm going to have to keep my job so that we can have a roof over our heads. Christ, he surely has fucked us over, Darling."

"I know." She hung up when he told her again that he had to go. She realized in that moment that she had no idea what it was he did for a living as it had never come up before. For all she knew, he could be an attorney who could get them out of this mess with her father, but she just didn't know. After all these years of marriage, she wasn't sure that it was a good time to ask him. Just go on pretending like she has forever. It had served her well, not knowing anything that was going on around her.

~*~

Dyson loved the big room that he'd been assigned. It was the master suite, one that had a big enough bed for him and Emma was on the second floor with Emitte in separate rooms. Standing at one of the biggest windows he'd ever seen, he looked around the backyard and marveled at the color of the trees that were there. The changing weather was making the backyard a wash of warm colors, and he could stare at it for hours and not see all of it.

"Can I talk to you?" He turned around and smiled at Emma. "I've just gotten off the phone with your sister-in-law, Amy. She said that we're married in the eyes of the court system, but that doesn't mean that we can't have a real wedding later. Why would she do that without asking?"

"I would say she thought that she was doing us a favor when it came to us having everyone believe that we're married already so there won't be any trouble with you using any credit cards that I've had made for you." He walked to one of the three dressers that were in the room. "Here you go. I meant to give them to you earlier. Also, you should know that your grandda had her put our names on the deed to this place and every other place that he owns and is leaving to you."

"To us. He's left everything to us. And speaking of which, he's decided that he wants immortality for a little while. He said that he wanted to wait around a bit and see if we have children so he can go back to his Sally, my grandma and tell her all the stories that he's come to be a part of. Did you want to have children someday?" He told her that he would like to have as many as she wanted. "I don't know how that is supposed to work. Do I have—speaking of dragons, there is one on my arm."

She showed him the little dragon that seemed to be clinging to her skin. After asking her if it hurt, she said that it didn't that she could feel him move when he did. Showing her his, a much larger dragon, he told her that he was there to protect her when she needed it. He mentioned a house fire and a car accident that his brother told him about. She didn't seem all that concerned about it but only nodded when he finished.

"Will we need to have sex at some point soon to bond? I have a wolf friend who told me that I'd be safer if we were to have sex. I don't know if I believe him or not, but he seemed to be sincere when he was telling me." Dyson told her that it was true, that she'd be stronger and have more magic. "I have that too. Magic now. I only just realized that I could change my clothing at will and that when I want something, a glass of something to drink, it's right there for me to enjoy. You're saying that I'll have more than that."

"A great deal more, as I've been told." She nodded and moved around the room. "I feel bad for taking this room from you. Are you sure you wouldn't be more comfortable up here and me take one of the smaller rooms?" She stood beside him without speaking and seemed to be engrossed in the window's view. "If you wanted, we could both sleep in here with separate beds if you'd like."

"I want to sleep with you. No sex right now. I've never slept with anyone before. But I would like to get used to having someone in the bed with me." He said that nothing would happen unless she wanted it to. "I'm glad to hear you say that. I'm not ready for sex just yet. I mean, we've only known one another for a few days. I'd like to get to know you by asking you questions about yourself and being a dragon." She looked up at him. "Can I see him? Now?"

"We'd have to go outside. I'm fairly large and would ruin the house if I were to shift into him. But I'd love for you to see him. I know that he's ready to show off for you." She turned and left him in the room. Dyson had to laugh. She wasn't one to waste words when she wanted something, and he liked that about her. Going down the stairs, she said she was going to the backyard there should be plenty of room out there for him to shift.

"My dragon can come to me in parts. What I mean is I can shift just my hand into him or bring out my tail a little. I don't have to shift all the way if that would be something that you'd like." Emma told him that she wanted to see his entire dragon. "All right. Just don't get too close to his tail. It's quite large and sometimes has a mind of its own. It's very sharp and could harm you. He won't want to, but it could happen."

Even though she said she wanted to see his entire dragon, he took his time in shifting. First, his body elongated, and then his great arms and legs. As each part of him moved to be his other half, Dyson was careful that she didn't seem frightened by him. When he was fully dragon, he laid down on the cool grass and watched her.

"You're beautifully scary, if that makes any sense." He told her that it did. That all his brothers were scary. But not so much as their mother was. "I would imagine that with her job as a time adjuster, she'd have to be large enough to shift the world around."

His mom and Aunt Ember, Mom's sister, had been time adjusters forever. They would go about the world, changing things that perhaps would take out a single person that might be needed in the future. Or his descendants. They were so good at it that there would never be that many flaws in the timeline that would have people confused. One time, his mother told him she'd had to make it so that a mountain didn't come down on a little town so that a child that his family would need later wouldn't die. They both did that until they met their mates. That, as a matter of fact, was how she'd met his dad.

"My father is a vampire and older than dirt. However, my mother is much older than him and can do things that not even my dad can do. Amy too. She has some traits of a vampire that is even older than Dad, and he's as proud of her as he is one of us. Dad loves all the women in the family." He told her how Amy could jump from flame to flame and move all over the world in just a few seconds. "She even saved my brother's life once when his head had nearly been removed."

When she started to walk around him, he made sure to keep his tail under control. His beast would sometimes wag his tail, much like a dog did when he was happy. He was careful not to swing it around too much and kill her. At the very least, hurt her in some way. When she came back to his head, she had a large scale of his.

"Does it hurt when you lose these?" He was so shocked that she had it in her hands that he didn't answer her right away. "I'm sorry. Should I have left it where it lay? I thought that you could put it back or something."

"No, I can't...Emma, those weigh nearly five thousand pounds each when they're fresh. And you just picked it up. They weigh a great deal less when they get dried out. That's what the faeries count on when they get one. For it to be flexible and easily cut down." She asked him if she could have one of them make her a bracelet of it. She had an idea that she needed it. "Whatever you wish, my love."

Calling to the faeries that were forever around, Emma explained to them what she wanted. They got to work right away on it and even on some of the pieces that they'd use for their homes. Roofs and doors. Sometimes, when the weather was bad, other shingles would blow off their homes but not dragon scales. They were perfect for keeping a home nice and warm. The faeries used them for other things, too, and were excited to have one that was so fresh so that they could cut it down.

It didn't take them long to cut down to size the bracelet that she wanted. Once it was put on her arm, one of the little people helped her seal it around her wrist. Asking her what she needed it for, she put her hand with the scale encircling her wrist into the air, and she was encased in scales that covered her from above her head to several inches into the ground. Nothing would be able to get to her if she were in trouble. Once the scales disappeared, she looked at him with a large smile. It did his heart good to see it.

"While I'm not sure of all the things that this can do, I know that it will protect me against anything that comes after me." He asked her if she could breathe all right. "I can. It's as if all the comforts of being in a room are right here for me. Light, air, and even a little cot that I can lay on while whatever is going on, I'll be rested."

While she sat in his palm, telling him what she could do with the scale of his, they watched the faerie cut down the scale in no time and fly away with its parts. The only thing that was left that hadn't been used was a small sliver of it that she picked up and showed him what she was going to have done with it.

"It'll be a beautiful gem for me to wear with my other piece. I think that I'll wear them when we go out to dinner. With all the colors that are around it, I'm betting that it will match anything that I wear. I just love it." He said that he'd make sure that if he had any more fall off, he'd make sure that she didn't want anything from it first. "No, the faeries get the most use out of it. They need it. I have everything that I need from your scales." She fingered the bracelet and told him how much she loved having a part of him with her at all times. He was going to have to think of something that he could get from her so that he had something similar when they weren't together. After a while, he realized that she'd fallen asleep in his hand, and he laid his own head down and watched her. She was perfection to him.

When the sun was fully down, he woke her so that he could shift into his other self. Walking hand in hand back into the house, he asked one of the little people to help out his mate by having a necklace made just for her. They were nearly falling all over themselves, wanting to help their new mistress. He knew when they were in the big bed together that, by morning, not only would she have what she wanted but that every one of the faeries had had some small hand in making it for her. Dyson again thought of how lucky he was to have such a wonderful mate as Emma Walsh in his life.

Chapter 5

Darling couldn't believe that her own father would leave her in the shape that he had. She didn't have any money now that he took back over his accounts. Her mortgage was passed due by several months — had she been paying the bank instead of buying new things for it she supposed that she'd be all right about now. But there were other things as well. The credit cards were overdue. There was no money in the bank, no savings to speak of, and she needed to have her hair and nails done last week. Nothing was going her way.

Deciding that she was going to go and talk to him, she went out to the garage to drive to his home. Of course, the car that she loved to drive was in the shop. For a little fender bender, they charged her well over four thousand dollars. And instead of billing her like they normally would have, because she'd not paid them the last time, she wasn't going to get anything fixed until she paid off the last fender bender that she'd had. Darling hated people. All of them.

Driving a stick shift was nothing that she'd ever learned how to do in her youth. So now that she was older, she couldn't believe that she was in her fifties now; she didn't want to learn a new thing this late in her life. Why they didn't make all the cars the same was beyond her. If they did that, she thought that people would buy more. But no one had ever asked her so she wasn't able to put her opinion in about it.

The drive over to his house, the Manor, shouldn't have taken her nearly an hour and a half. But every time she stopped for a light or something, she'd forget to put it in the first gear. If that wasn't enough, she'd forget to put her foot on the brake, and the car would leap forward, scaring ten years off her life every time. By the time she got to the Manor, she was exhausted and a mess. The top had been down on the car, and since she didn't know how to put it back up, she had to drive all the way there with it down and it had made her hair look a fright. While blaming it on Emma wasn't really fair, she did so with every stop, studder, and leap that she made. Cursing the younger woman all the drive to her father's house.

For whatever reason, she couldn't get the car to drive up the drive. It would leap forward and then stop like there was some kind of wall in front of her. And wouldn't you know it, the man at the gate, she'd forgotten about there being someone out there, he said that he couldn't help her if she couldn't get by the magic.

Magic? Not believing in magic had served her well all her life. But now that she was faced with it, not being able to get into the drive to her family home, she had to think why this particular magic was keeping her from talking to her father. There had to be some way that she could get to him and get things straightened out. She pulled out her cell phone.

"Father, I can't get up the driveway. The man you have at the gate said that it's magic. Whatever. Tell him to let me through so that we can talk about this letter I got yesterday." He said 'no'. Nothing else but no. "What do you mean no? Father, this isn't going to bode well for you. I need to talk to you. And if you think that you're leaving all your wealth to Emma and Poppy, then you'd better be rethinking that, too."

"You're wrong about me leaving my things to Emma and Poppy. I believe I made it crystal clear that I'm not leaving Poppy anything. I've asked you this before and it bares repeating, what sort of name is Poppy anyway? Who did you name her after." She told him that she'd name her after him. "My name isn't Poppy either, you old fool. My name is Emitte Marshall. I don't even have a middle name."

"I know that. I called you Pop when I was a child. I thought that you'd like her better if I named her after you." He pointed out to her again that his name wasn't Poppy or Pop. "Father, this is not a conversation to have on the phone. Just tell the man that I'm allowed to come up to the house from now on, and we won't have to have a conversation about how you're treating me."

"I've already answered that. No. And he's not forbidding you from coming up. There is real magic there that keeps anyone with ill will in their heart from coming up to the house and doing terrible things. If you want to know the truth, Darling, I never expected you to get this close. I wish we would have had that sooner. Your mother might well still be alive. I know you killed her off, Darling. Just proving it has been a hardship." She was too shocked to say anything to him about her mother. She had killed her but didn't know that her father was looking into it. "Now, as I was telling you, no, you're not going to be coming up here. We're settling in just fine and dandy and don't need any of your trouble up here while we do it. Why don't you get yourself a job, Darling? Most people with debt as large as you do have to get one."

"I don't want a job. I want you to keep taking care of me the way you've always done. This is all Emma's fault, isn't it? She's convinced you to take me out of your will so that she can have it all." He told her that she didn't need it. "Of course she does. Everyone needs money. The more, the better."

"It just so happens that she's gone and married

herself up with one of them Walsh men. Got more money than they can count, I've heard." She sputtered about that, not believing for a moment that someone had more money than they needed. Or could count. "I gotta go, Darling. You've wasted enough of my time and I have things I need to get done. I'm having the whole house done up so that it's a might friendlier than it was when you lived here. You have yourself a good life now. Or don't. I don't care one lick if you do or not."

When he hung up on her, she held the phone to her ear, yelling at him to come back to her. The nerve of him. What the hell was he thinking about hanging up on her? Darling put her phone in her purse. She was fearful of what the phone company had said when she broke it the last time. She wasn't going to be getting any more free phones because she kept tossing them across the room.

The man at the gate, she'd never bothered with getting his name, told her that she was going to have to move on and that others were coming in. She didn't want to move but was afraid that he'd have her arrested or something. That would just be the candle on her cake today.

It took her four tries to get the car turned around and another twenty minutes of her trying to get the stupid thing to go forward so that she could get out of the drive. She couldn't see who was in the car behind her, but she just knew that it was either Emma or that rich husband of hers. Not that she believed that it was the Walshs that she married into, but she just didn't know what to believe anymore. Everyone was lying to her.

Sorting through her credit cards she found one that she'd taken out in Emma's name that she'd applied for. Going to have her hair and nails done was such a treat for her that she was nearly giddy with excitement. Once she was seated, they asked her how she was paying.

"With a credit card." The woman, someone that she didn't know, put out her hand for it. "You can't charge me before we even get started. That's not fair." Still, her hand was out. "You can bet that I'm not going to tip you after this either. This isn't right. If you must know, my sister gave me her credit card so that I could have a pamper day."

Finally handing over the card, she asked whose name it was in. Of course, the woman took it away, and before she could come back to her with the card, her cell phone rang. It was Emma the bitch.

"That's not going to work for you. I don't have any idea how you did that with my name on the card, but I've asked the young woman who took it from you to tear it up. Why on earth would you think that I would allow you a pamper day when I don't even like you." She told her that was harsh and unnecessary. "Be that as it may, I can't stand you, and I'm not going to be paying for you to have shit done to you. As Grandda had said to you, get a job. Oh, speaking of which, David is going to lose his job today. Did you know that he's been taking from the petty cash for the last several months to supply you with money to go on your little tantrums? Or whatever he calls having to give you money so that you aren't pissy with him when he comes home. That's a big no-no in any job. Whatever will you do now?"

"You're a liar." She asked her why that was the first thing someone said when they didn't want to hear what you were saying to them? "I don't know. But you are a liar about David. He's a good attorney, and he knows how much him having a job means to me. To us."

"Yes, well, that bird has flown." Half the time, she didn't understand Emma. She had hung out with her father too much and sounded just like him all the time. Damn it to hell and back. What was this world coming to when everyone was against her?

Not even waiting for the woman to come back with the card, she gathered her purse and headed out to the car. She was there just in time to see it being loaded onto a large truck and being strapped down. Asking the driver, a burly-looking man, what he thought he was doing, he said that she was going to take it up with Shuttle and Shuttle, the law firm on Main. She knew where that was, but she didn't understand why they'd be taking her car from her. Pulling out her phone when it rang, she nearly screamed at the picture showing there.

"What has happened, David? You told me that your job was in the bag." He told her what Emma had said, that he'd been taking from petty cash. "Isn't that what it's there for? For someone to use when they're running low?"

"Running short, not low. I used all twenty grand of it. And when they had an audit done on my cases, they took a look at that as well." He spoke to someone else before coming back to her. "How the hell did you find out already? I didn't even have time to call you."

"I don't know how she found out, but Emma told me the same thing. What are we going—why are they taking my car? How the hell am I supposed to be able to get around without something to drive from now on."

"The company owns all three of our cars, including the one that I drove to work today. They've already been to the house to change the locks." She asked him why they were doing that. "They lent me the money to purchase the house and since I've never made a payment on it, apparently, they're taking it and the contents too. They're not even going to let us get anything personal from the house as they said that I owe them that, too. Why did they say that I've never made a payment on the house, Darling?" She changed the subject.

"What am I supposed to do to get back to the house. And they will, too, allow me to get things from that house, or I'll call the police on them. There is no way they have the right to do anything of the kind, David. You tell them that." He asked about the mortgage. "So I missed a few payments. It's not like it's the end of the world. Christ, they can well afford it."

"They're saying that I've missed every payment and balloon payment. Christ, what the fuck did you do with all that money? You couldn't have been getting your hair and nails done that much, could you?" She told him to get back on the subject of her. "You know, it's always been about you, hasn't it? No matter what I do, it is all centralized on you and what you want. You know what? I'm kind of glad this has happened. Now I can start fresh without you and that damned daughter of yours. Christ, when I think of all the money...You didn't make a single payment when you assured me that you had been."

When he hung up on her without even saying goodbye, she wanted to call him back and tell him there was no need for him to be rude. But she saw Emma, and she made her way across the street, not even watching the street for cars. She nearly got herself killed by simply plowing across to her. Darling completely ignored the man who was with her.

"You've done this." Emma didn't even try to deny it. She just smiled at her like a simpleton. "My husband is out of work. I don't have a car to get home and speaking of which, they think that they're going to take that as well."

"You should be better with your money, I guess." When she turned her back on her to leave, Darling saw red. Her body stiffened up so tightly that she could feel her head pounding with the anger that she had. Reaching for her, going to jerk her around, all she ended up with was her arm jerked up behind her and in more pain than she'd ever been in her life. "Don't. Touch. Me."

"You're hurting me. Let me go, and when you do so, you know I'm going to slap the piss right out of you. Let me the fuck go." Her arm was pulled tighter until she was on the ground. When she heard the pop, then the pain, it was all she could do to remain conscious. She did scream when she was let go.

"You mother fucker, you hurt me." Instead of yelling more, Darling leaned over to her side and puked up her breakfast. It wasn't any better coming out than it had been doing down. She hated oatmeal but needed it as badly as her dad did. "I'm going to have you arrested. See that I don't."

"I'm not worried about you anymore, Darling. To be honest, I'm not worried about Poppy or David either. For the first time in a long time, I'm happy and doing what I want. Grandda is going to outlive you and your family, and I think that's wonderful." She told her to fuck off. "Brave words for someone who has just gotten their arm dislocated and can't get a ride to the hospital or home — not that you have one. I think I'll buy it just to see what sort of shit you have in that house you had. I hope you rot in hell."

Someone called the police, for which she was grateful, but they took entirely too long to get her an ambulance. She was hurting so badly by the time she got there that all she wanted to do was be knocked out. There were several people there who were willing to do it for her — people that she'd dealt with before, but finally, she was given something and let it roll over her. She could plot Emma's demise later. Right now, she was in too much pain to even think about where she was going to rest her head tonight.

~*~

That night, when the two of them went to bed, she wasn't as exhausted as she had been before. She was more aware of him being in the bed with her. More aware of his chill, too. She turned to ask him about how he could be so cold and a dragon too.

"We're cold-blooded. All of us are." He pulled her back to him, but she escaped so that she could at least warm herself up a little before falling asleep. "If you would just let me get a little warmer, then I'll be all right. I can get another blanket if you wish."

"Yes, please." He left the bed, and she shivered. It was like it was ten below in the room, and she didn't think that she'd be able to sleep at all. When the second thick blanket was over her, she tried to keep as far from Dyson as she could. Christ, he was so cold that she thought it might be warmer outside. And it was in the sixties out there.

"Did I tell you that Layla is the fire starter for our kind?" He was rubbing his hand up and down her back. It felt better, but she was still chilled. "She is the one that will give new hatchlings their fire or whatever they need when they're big enough to handle their flame. It might not be fire. It could be ice or wind, too. I don't know any dragons that can breathe wind, but my mom said that it's hurricane-like and has been known to topple buildings and sink ships it's so strong."

"What about the ice dragons? I mean, how does that work?" He explained to her how dragons, with their icy cold breath, could kill a man in an instant. "Do they look like regular dragons? I mean, how will I know which kind they are if I were to see them?"

"They look like regular dragons but for their breath and beard. You'll notice first that they have a beard on their chin that is made of ice. Their eyes are silver, too. They are not really silver in color but like ice when you look at them. And since they're ice cold all the time, I mean, like when they rest as their dragons, they form a protective shell around them that is solid ice. When they move suddenly, the ice around them flies off and kills those around them. They're very dangerous dragons even when they're not in fighting mode."

"I'm assuming that breathing air is dangerous too. Can they blow wind or whatever it's called over water and make it devour the lands surrounding it?" He said that was just what they did. "Getting the three kinds of dragons together much be a terrible day for weather."

"Those aren't the only three kinds of dragons. Just the most dangerous. There are colored dragons as well. I'm a green dragon, as you noticed. My brother Fowler is a red dragon. He has the hottest heat of us all. The rest of us are blue dragons. We all should have been, but Mom thinks that because there is some vampire in our line, that's what changed me to green. I have green eyes as well like the others have blue." She said that she'd never noticed that before. "Mom has blue eyes. Very dark and almost look black. When she's her dragon, she's bigger than the rest of us, too, with the exception of Fowler. Since he's the leader of our group, he's bigger than our mom by a little."

When he started massaging her shoulders, she felt herself relaxing. The bed was warmer now, and she wanted to lean back into him. But she knew better. Just because the bed was warm, it didn't mean that he was warm yet. She was going to have to ask the other wives how they were tolerant of the cold bed. They had to be doing something different than she was.

He told her of the different colored dragons. Most of them were blue and green, a normal color for them. But there were ones that had diamond scales on them that made them blend into the things around them, thus keeping them from being seen. Then he told her about the other realm.

"My great-grandmother was the queen when I was born. I didn't know until recently why she was asked to step down. I always thought that she'd gotten tired of the job. Grandma Morning got bored, too, and turned it over to my mom. But anyway, she was asked to step down because she was taking money from people in order for them to pay their way out of trouble. She used that money to fund this dragon by the name of Grail. Now, there was a terrible dragon. He was black." She turned in the bed and looked up at Dyson while he told the story of his family. "Great-Grandma didn't care for being asked to step down, so she devised a plot that would kill Fowler by having Grail removed his head. Her plan was that since he was so well-loved and the oldest of the children, everyone would be in a state of mourning. While we were having our hearts broken, she and Grail had planned to move into the other realm and take over. Their plan was to kill off all the dragons but for the two of them and form their own magic."

"Would that work? I was to understand that if there are no dragons, then there isn't any magic. Isn't that right?" Dyson told her that was exactly right. "Then I don't understand how that was going to work if there was no more magic."

"You're right and thinking better than they did. You see, they nearly did kill off Fowler. And if not for the help of Amy, his mate, then he would have died right then. But there was just a flap, they called it, of his neck still attached to his head and she put it back on his neck where it sealed up. Then, she killed Grail. She did that by putting both her hands, which were covered in flames, to his head and burnt it right off his shoulders. For her to have been able to do that was unheard of. But she did it, and in a huge ceremony to write her name in the Book of Dragons, we were all together. When Grannie, what we've all been calling her since she was dead, found out about it, she took the sword of fire starter and nearly killed Amy with it. Instead, Fowler changed into his great beast and removed her head with one bite. That destroyed the trouble that we'd been having all along, and we've been happier since." He laughed a little. "It was a great deal more dramatic than that, but you get the picture, I think."

She was so relaxed by the time he'd finished with his story that she was nearly asleep. Dyson's body had finally warmed up enough that she could be close to him, so she felt her body, already close to sleep, relax even more, she turned in the bed so that he had his chest to her back. He knew that if he moved his legs, even enough to wrap around hers, she would wake again as he was that cold, so he just thought about what it was going to be like in the winter months and his body even colder.

Since he'd never heard his brothers' mates complaining about the cold, he was going to have to ask them about it. Knowing Fowler, who seemed to be as cold as he was all the time, he more than likely had a plan that didn't have his wife seeking other places to sleep because of the chill he gave all. Making a mental note about it, he knew that he'd do it in the morning.

Two days ago, he'd found the ring that Sidney had made when he was in his jewelry making phase of his life. That was another thing that Dyson hadn't ever gotten into was: gem making. But Sidney had excelled at it. Not only did he make rings and other jewelry, but he also made stained glass windows that were still to this day in churches and very large houses.

His favorite piece that he'd ever seen of his brothers was the one that was in their home front door. It was several dragons, some of them standing, the rest sitting on the emerald green grass of the lawn. It was so beautiful that when Mom decided to change the porch and front room one year, she had him add to the mural by extending the scene to the front windows of the house too. Dyson was going to talk to his brother about making a piece for his new home so that he'd have a little bit of his family there with him at all times.

Just as he was thinking that he was tried enough to go to sleep, he remembered wanting to take Emma to the gem cave. All the gems that they'd all made were there. Some of them had been separated out by gem, but for the most part, they were just scattered about the large cave like someone had just stood at the door and tossed them in. Dyson knew that his mother had a large basket that she kept her tears in or any that she might well find and took them to the cave when the basket was full. She, he knew, had given up about keeping them in any kind of order and he loved to hear her complain about how they were just everywhere.

As a child, he remembered his dad saying that

if a human were to find the cave, they'd die from the riches there. No human could nor would be able to comprehend the amount of wealth that had been hidden away there, and that had been hundreds of years ago. He wouldn't know how to calculate a number of what was there now. He was sure that it was enough to make every human in the world wealthy beyond their wildest dreams.

Snuggling down into his pillow, he thought about how Emma had accepted his dragon. He might not have been able to shift and save her like his older brother had, but he thought that she understood that he and his beast were there for her if she needed them. To be able to have her touching him and then wanting a piece of his dragon, Dyson thought himself to be the luckiest dragon that had ever been hatched. She loved him no matter what he looked like, and that was more than enough for him.

Just as he was falling to sleep he thought once more about the trouble that they were going to have with Darling and her family. He was glad on so many levels that he was able to keep his new family safe, but still worried about them getting too close to her. He'd have to keep better care to be around Emma all the time. It was time he thought to employee some extra faeries. They would literally die for her and while he didn't want that, he did want his mate safe. Tomorrow, he was going to talk to his grandma and see what she could do to help him out. There were just too many things that could go wrong with having humans around. They were too sneaky at best, and he never understood their need to kill people. Yes, he thought, he needed to go to the other realm and see about getting help. He'd also take Emma with him so that she could look at all the animals that he'd bet she thought were not real.

Wide awake now, he thought of having a nice picnic in the other realm. He knew that he'd not done that in a long time. Hanging out with the unicorns would be a blast for Emma. There were other animals that she'd enjoy, too, like the small pixies and brownies. They didn't spend all that much time in this realm as they were considered to be troublemakers.

They were, for some reason, really good at keeping the trolls in line. He was so excited that he nearly wrapped his legs around Emma's but caught himself just in time. All he needed to do now was wake her up from her sleep and have to hear about how cold he was making her. He'd love it having her fuss at him, but she would be upset and he didn't want that. Not when he was making such plans with her in mind.

Maybe an electric blanket would be good for them. Or perhaps a fireplace in the room. Whatever was making the other mates warm, he needed to find out. Dyson didn't want his mate suffering at all if there

Kathi S. Barton

was something that he could do about it.

Chapter 6

She couldn't help but stare at the room. It was almost too hot with all the heat coming from different points in the room. There were two fireplaces that she was sure hadn't been there before. Several blankets on the bed that looked like they were electric blankets as there were cords running to the outlets that, again, she'd not noticed before. And in the middle of the room was the biggest basket of fruit that she'd ever seen in her life.

"What is all this?" He grinned. "You know, you're not as charming as you might think that you are. What have you done?"

"I wanted to keep you sleeping with me, so I figured out what I needed, and the faeries helped me out. I'm sure that now when we go to bed, you won't have to be chilled sleeping with me." She just stared at him. "All right. I went to talk to my brothers, Fowler and Madison and they said that they've never had any trouble with being too cold for their mates. I asked my grandma and she said that it had to do with me being different than them. As I said to you once, Fowler is a red dragon, which makes him hotter than any of us.

Being a green dragon and different than them, I guess that I'm colder than any of them."

"How do you suppose making the room hot will make you warmer?" He told her that he didn't know, but he was willing to try anything to make her happy. "I am happy, Dyson. Just having you in my life has made me the happiest that I've ever been."

"Thank you. I needed to hear that. There is another theory as to how to warm us up. It's not anything that I'm going to pressure you into, but Grandma said that if we were to mate and have sex, then it would more than likely mellow out between us." He felt his face heat up, and he smiled at her. "Making love to you would be the greatest thing, but I'm not going to pressure you into anything just to make you want to sleep with me."

Before he could think her intentions, she came to him and put her hands on his chest. He knew she felt his heart. He could, as well. It was pounding hard beneath her hands. Beating hard because she touched him. When she licked her lips, running her tongue over their fullness, Dyson leaned in to kiss her.

The kiss was gentle. He didn't want to frighten her. The touching of their bodies seemed to melt into one. It didn't matter that he was chilled. She seemed to warm him up from his core to his skin.

As he brought her closer to him, his hands

holding her tightly to him, Dyson felt something that he'd never felt before. A connection to another person on a level that he'd only felt with his family but on a different level than he'd ever felt before. Lifting her up in his arms, he turned her to the wall behind them and felt her wrap around him.

"I can't wait," he told her when he pulled his mouth free. "I need to bury myself deep inside of you. I need to make you mine."

Nodding, she began to tear at his clothing. It was the most erotic thing that he'd ever felt. His shirt was jerked open, tearing the buttons off as she touched his skin. His jacket was pulled down over his arms and dropped where it lay.

Her own clothing suffered as much as his did. The blouse she had on was ripped open. The black bra that seemed sexy for the moment he saw it was lifted up, and he pulled her breast into his mouth. Tugging at her pants, he nearly cried out when they caught. But finally, in the end, he simply tore them from her, no longer caring to be careful of what she would wear later.

"Hurry." He grinned at her urgency. He, too, felt it, the need to mate, to become one. When his pants gave him fits, he pulled a little of his beast, and the pants fell away in shreds. His feet were now bare of shoes and socks as he held her naked body close to his.

While he wasn't sure how he'd come to be naked, he didn't care so long as he could be inside of Emma.

"I want to see you." Her head shook, and he pulled her legs from behind him. "I must see you in all your glory. We, my dragon and I, we need it. Need to see the beauty that we know that you are."

"I'm not that special. I'm sorry, but I don't want to disappoint you." He had her standing before him now, her body beautifully bare and his. "You're so large, aren't you. I'm a little afraid that you're going to...I don't care. I want you, Dyson."

He looked down at his own body and saw himself as she might. His cock was thick and hard, straining from his body with pre-cum at the tip, dripping off the tip. His chest was wide, devoid of hair, and his nipples, like hers, were hard. Dyson wanted to taste every part of her, drink from her nectar, and hear her scream out his name. But he needed to be inside of her more than his need to satisfy his need for a drink.

"I want you in a way that I've never wanted anything in my life, Emma. Feel you tighten around me as I fill you." She nodded, and he put out his finger to trace her collarbone to her nipple. "The thought of fucking you has my beast snarling at me to begin, but I want to give you pleasure first."

"If you do this right, I'm going to have a great deal of pleasure, I think." Her hand slipped over her mouth when she spoke, and he pulled it away. "I don't know why I said that."

"Yes, you do. You are as needy as I am." Dyson ran his finger down her belly to her navel and then played there for a moment. Her moans had him watching her face, and he almost missed what her fingers were doing.

They were at her pussy, just above her nether lips, but so very close that he wanted to beg her to dip them inside. Sliding his own fingers to match with hers, he felt the heat of her pull at him when he gently parted her lips for her own fingers.

"I need to taste you." He dropped to his knees and licked her fingers clean after pulling them free of her soft, nether lips. Sucking her clit into his mouth and then biting down gently, he was rewarded with a mouthful of her cream and the first taste of paradise. Lifting her leg up to get to his feast, Dyson ate her like he'd wanted to his entire life, he thought.

"Please. I'm going to fall." Her voice was weak, her body trembling when he helped her to the floor. But as soon as she was there, he knew it was time to have her. Sliding up her body, he suckled at her breast until her legs came up around his hips, and his cock was at her entrance.

Her heat pulled at him. There was nothing holding him back but for her permission. Christ, he wanted her so bad, his body suddenly burning with the need to take her. Looking her in the eyes, he knew it was now or never.

"You belong to us. No one but us." She only stared up at him, his beast telling him to take her. "Tell me, Emma. Tell me you belong to us."

"I don't know what that means." He moved into her, the crown of his cock filling her the way he wanted to his entire body. "Please, take me."

"Say it. I need to hear you say it." Emma moaned when he moved in and out of her again, just the tip of his cock making her beg for more. "Christ, I need you. I need you to tell me you belong to us."

"I belong to you and your dragon. Now take me." He filled her with his cock. And his heart, too. As he took her, feeling her body accepting his and the dragon, he knew that, on some level, there would be no turning back from this. And he didn't want to.

When he cupped her ass to his body, pulling her clit and her pussy tightly against his groin, she screamed out his name, telling him over and over that she was theirs. Dyson felt his own climax take him, the beast within him coming as well. And when he leaned into her throat to make her his, his dragon took him a little, and they both tasted their mate's blood.

The room darkened around them. He couldn't see, couldn't breathe for what had just happened.

When she moaned beneath him, Dyson looked at his mate and felt warmth fill him. Her body, her heart they were his just as much as he belonged to her.

Dyson held her to him as she lay limp beneath him. Rolling to his back, keeping her safely in his arms, he thought of what they'd just done, and he was good with it. Licking the wound closed at her throat, he held her to him, protecting her, warming her as he would for the rest of his days.

He woke later in the night. His body was sore, but he attributed that to them sleeping on the floor. Rolling as gently as he could from beneath her, he stood up and moaned at the pain that was throughout his body. Picking Emma up and putting her to bed, he went to the bathroom to use the toilet. On his way back, he turned off the heaters and the electric blankets and got into bed with her.

"You're so warm." He felt it, too. Like his body was as toasty warm as her body was. When she wrapped herself around him, Dyson thought for sure that he could take on the world at that moment and come out on top. It was a wonderful feeling to have his mate with him as he drifted off to sleep.

The next time he woke, the room was flooded with bright light. The bed covers were at the bottom of the bed and he reached for the sheet to cover himself up when he realized that Emma was no longer in bed with him. Reaching out beyond the room he was in, he found her in the bathroom taking a shower. Thinking of joining her, he leapt out of bed and fell to the floor.

Every part of his body was in pain, and he didn't think that even the best doctors in the world could ever make him feel like a man again. Whimpering as quietly as he could, he crawled on his hands and knees to the side of the bed to use it to get to his feet again. He was dying. He just knew it.

"Are you all right?" He looked at Emma when she spoke from the doorway to the bathroom. "You look like I felt when I got up. If I hadn't of had to pee so bad, I would have gone back to bed and not moved again. Take a shower. You'll feel better."

"I can't move." He heard the whining in his voice but didn't care. This was her fault for making love to him and nearly killing him. "How are you even moving around right now?"

"I told you. Take a shower, and you'll feel like a human...well, whatever you are. Get going. I have some things that I need to talk to you about. I have this huge assed dragon on my back, and he keeps moving around me." She turned around, and he could see the green dragon on her back.

It was huge for her tiny frame, and its claws were in her shoulders and hips like he was literally clinging to her. Getting up, already feeling a little better, he limped his way to her and touched his fingers to the head of the thing.

"Do you have one too?" He turned and that was when he felt the dragon on his own back. His was larger, of course, but it was clinging to him in the same way. His tail, filled with dangerous-looking horns, was wrapped around his leg and ended at his feet. When he moved, just climbing a little higher on his back, he felt it like it was a part of him. "I can hear it talking."

Her whispered comment had him realizing that he could hear it as well. While he was sure they were talking to each other, he really didn't understand what they were saying. It wasn't until he touched his hand to Emma's lower back that he could understand them. They really were talking to each other.

"They're getting acquainted. Can you hear them?" Emma told him that she could now, that she could understand them as well. "I know about them. At least I heard my brother talking to Sidney, I think it was that we'd all get one when we found our mates. They're there to protect us from harm. I'm not entirely sure how that works but that's what I heard. We'll each get one when our mates come along. And I suppose bond with them."

"We need to write this shit down for future generations." He agreed and moved around her to go to the bathroom. "I need to bring some of my things here so that when I shower, I don't smell all manly. Also, you might want to forgo the loofa sponge on your back. I don't think the dragons care for that all that much. He bit the one I was using in half."

He burst out laughing when she finished. She told him that like it was an everyday occurrence for them to have to tussle with a dragon that was on their backs. Dyson didn't tell her that he didn't care for a loofa anyway but smiled when he thought of the picture she must have made fighting with a dragon on how she wanted to have her back cleaned.

After getting out of the shower and dressing, Dyson had to admit that he did feel much better. There were twinges when he moved a certain way, but other than that, he thought that the worst was over. For now, at least. Making his way to the kitchen, he could hear voices before he entered the room.

~*~

Emma watched as her step-sister Darling made her way to her. She'd been agreeable to meet with the older woman, but she'd already decided that she wasn't going to put up with any shit from her. She was in a great mood and didn't want her to mess that up for her. Who knew that making love with someone that you loved could make a person feel so good. Darling sat down with a huff.

"I'm ordering anything I want, and you're

going to foot the bill. I've been staying at the local bed and breakfast too that I expect you to pa — where are you going? I'm not nearly finished with you." She told her that she wanted this meeting on the condition that she didn't ask for money. "I didn't ask for shit. I said you were going to pay for it. Now, sit down and shut up. I have things to talk over with you."

Emma sat, but she didn't think she'd be there much longer. When the waiter came to take their order, she smiled at him. The poor man was in for a rude table guest, and she wanted so badly to tell him that he'd still get a tip from her.

Darling ordered herself a steak, which they didn't have on the lunch menu. She had to settle for a burger and fries. But she did tell the man that she was going to come by tonight to get her steak dinner and that it would be paid for. She also ordered something to go with her, like a second burger and also several desserts. When he turned to her, she could see that his smile was tight.

"I'm paying, and I'm only paying for the burger she's having now. Nothing to go, nor will I pay for the steak she thinks she's coming in later to get. Do you understand?" He said that he did and marked through some things on his paper. "I'll have a burger as well and double the French fries."

After he left them to get their drink orders,

Emma smiled at Darling. There was so much hatred on her face it was almost as if she was going to have a stroke or something. Smiling at her again, feeling like she was in a better position than she'd been in her life, Emma asked her what she wanted to talk about.

"Money. I know that I'm not to ask you for any, so I'm going to demand that you give me what I have coming from the estate." Emma told her no, that she wasn't going to do that. "You will, or I'm going to make your life a living hell."

"You're already doing that now. But I'm better prepared now, and you'll find that I'm not so easily manipulated anymore. I'm a stronger person than I was even a week ago." Their drinks were brought, and the waiter told her that her husband was here. Would he be alright to sit with them? Darling said no. "Yes, please have him come and sit with us. I had hopes that he'd make it."

"This meeting is between the two of us." She pointed out that as loud as she was being, everyone knew what was going on. "I'll yell if I want to if that's what it takes for you to give me what is rightfully mine. You stole it all from me, and I demand that you return it to me posthaste."

Dyson sat with them and kissed her. She was amazed every time that he touched her that he was all hers. Looking at her step-sister and wondered why she'd even agreed for this to happen. Today, of all days when she was feeling like a million bucks. Before she could speak to Darling, even if she thought that she could get through to her, Dyson spoke.

"First of all, you cannot collect on the will of a man that is still alive. When I left Emitte just a little bit ago, he was playing chess with my dad. When he dies, and I don't see that happening for a long time yet, you can say whatever you want about my wife getting his estate. But she will inherit it from him, again, when he dies." She told Dyson that she knew she wasn't going to get any of it. "Not our problem. Perhaps had you been a better person than you are then he might have left you something. When he dies. From what I am to understand, you took from him all your life. Not just stealing things from the house but money, too. I don't think that you're going to get anything else from him or the estate, even if you were to change yourself around. As of two weeks ago, the house and all the land that surrounded it were signed over to myself and Emma. That means when he dies, the estate won't be as —"

"You can't have that, it's mine. Damn you, Emma, I should have killed you rather than send you over to my parents to be their peon. The things that you've done...I want what is rightfully mine, damn you." Emma waited until the waiter was gone, dropping off not only their burgers but one for Dyson as well. She shared her fries with him as well. "I'm going to sue you. That's what I'm going to do. David will have you in court in—"

"Sorry, but David no longer has the right to be called an attorney. When he was caught stealing— something that seems to run in your family—then he is no longer allowed to practice law anywhere. He gave up his license rather than face jail time. Didn't he tell you that?" Emma laughed as she took a bite of her burger. When she was finished eating her bite, she looked at Darling again. "You really fucked up, I'm afraid. Nothing is coming to you once Grandda passes away. However, I have a feeling that he's going to be around much longer than you'll be."

"I wouldn't count on that. Mother didn't make it, thanks to me. And it's doubtful that he will for much longer. I'm going to take you to court as soon as I get out of this place." She stood up then and drew in a deep breath. "Do you all hear me? I'm going to sue this bitch for her taking what is rightfully mine."

No one even turned in her direction. It was as if they had gotten used to her yelling, and it didn't bother them anymore. Before she left, however, Darling reached over and grabbed her still-uneaten hamburger. She thought for sure that she was going to take it with her, but she actually tossed it in their direction. It didn't hit them as a sudden shield was in front of the two of them.

Emma was still laughing an hour later when Darling had been arrested. Since she couldn't get her food on them, she went to other tables and tossed other patrons' food at them. Dyson just ate his burger like there wasn't anything amiss. She just laughed. It was, by far, the funniest thing that she'd ever seen. A grown woman having a temper tantrum in the middle of a posh restaurant like she was a two year old without a nap.

"That was a great burger. And the show that was going on around us was the best." She giggled, telling Dyson that she'd enjoyed it as well. "We'll have to go back again if they allow us to and have their soup and salad. The loaded baked potato soup looks like something that I'd enjoy."

They talked about silly things on the way back to the house. She told him that she'd thought it was funny how someone had to point out to Darling that in order to collect from a reading of the will, someone had to actually die first.

Grandda had decided that he wanted to hang around a few more decades just to outlive Darling. He said that he wanted to dance on her headstone just once and then be done with her. She was going to bring the music and take pictures.

They were also looking to have her mom's

body exhumed. After Darling left, announcing how she'd been the one that had killed Grandma Sally, the owner of the restaurant had offered them a copy of the recording so that she could take it to the police to have them look into it. It broke her heart and that of her grandda to know that Darling had stooped so low as to kill her own mother.

"Why do you call them your grandda and grandma when they're really your parents? I've meant to ask you that before, but I never found the right time." She told him what she'd told them when they adopted her. "So you called them your grandparents because that was something that pissed off Darling more than you calling them Mom and Dad. I guess I can understand that. When a lot of people were calling your parents Mom and Dad for the fun of it, it was really the grandparent's angle that set her ass on fire. I don't know if you know this or not but Emitte has asked me to call him that as well. He thinks of us more as his grandchildren than his children. Because of the age difference, I suppose."

"Grandda loves you so much, Dyson. As much as I do, I think." He told her that he loved her as well. "Good. Now, I've talked to Amy and she told me that we can have a baby whenever I'm ovulating. I've stopped taking the pill. She told me that it wouldn't work anyway if we decided to have a few children. I'm excited."

"I am as well. To see you large with one of our children will make my life complete. They'll be dragons. You're aware of that, correct?" She told him that she was, again, Amy had told her. "She read the dragon book, both of them when she and Fowler got together. She knows a lot of rules that no one has enforced for a very long time."

"I can see her doing that. Keeping up with the rules that would govern all of you guys. She even explained to me a bit better about Layla being the fire starter, too. I hadn't any idea that you weren't born with your breath until it was given to you." He told her that he'd not either until it had been explained to him. "Your kind, they're very secretive, aren't you? I mean, I wish that I could see the sky darken with the dragons as your mother and father had. I love seeing you be able to fly with your brothers in the other realm."

"We'll have to go back there soon. I enjoyed showing you around when we were there the other day. I was seeing things in a way that you might see things. Like the unicorns and other flying creatures." Emma reminded him that her favorite part was the flowers and the way they were cared for. "Yes, I know that you made a few friends with the brownies, too. I think they'd save you over me now."

"That's the way it should be, too." They both

laughed, walking around hand in hand and greeting people. "It's getting chillier now. But I can go to bed and be warm now. Who knew that it took an entire night of debilitating sex to make you warm-blooded. We'll have to do that soon again so that we can see what else sex can do to you."

"Have you figured out any more magic? I know that you've found a few things you can do." She asked him if he'd been told about the flame that she has, much like Amy has. "She told me. I think that it's wonderful that you can bounce right to me or disaster when you're needed. And it does happen where we go in under cover of darkness and help with fires that are taking over entire states. The firefighters do a great job and work harder than any department that I know of, but they get exhausted, too, and it's our pleasure to go in and help them out."

Emma spoke to him about the other things that she could do. It didn't take her long to figure out that she could heat stones to put near plants to keep the frost from killing them. The faeries loved that, too. And that she could, without any muscle work at all, lift things up and move them, such as cars and trucks. He asked her what use that would have.

"I don't know yet. But I'm sure that since I have it, I'll need it. I did move things around in the barn that is out back. Grandda wanted some of the tractors moved so that he could get to the cellar. I didn't even know there was one in the barn until he mentioned it. Now he wants to go down there and see what treasures might have been stored there." He told her that there might be damage to things because of the mice. "Yes, I guess we won't have any trouble with mice anymore with you guys around either. Odd thing, I think. For a tiny mouse to be afraid of a giant dragon."

Dinner wasn't going to be for a few more hours so they decided to go out into the yard to put the ground flowers to sleep. It wasn't that hard, not with the help of the earthly creatures, but she couldn't wait for the flowers to start popping their heads up above the straw that they would keep warm in when it started to be warmer all the time. She was looking forward to spring and summer like she hadn't before.

After dinner, the two of them sat in the living room with grandda. He was in such a good mood that she didn't bring up the meeting with Darling or the exhumation of Grandma Sally. When he got on the subject of the barn and how she was able to help him up in getting to the lower level, he told them the things that were down there.

"Barrels of things that had been packed away so long ago that I don't remember what's in them anymore. I know that they're marked and all, but it's difficult to read what it says. My mom was good at getting barrels for packing things away. She said that the mice would be too drunk after chewing on the wood to be able to get into the nice things in them. Sometimes I have to remind myself that you're not blood related to her but I swear to you, you act just like her at times, Emma. Sometimes I even hear you say something, more than likely you've heard it from me that reminds me of her. I so love you, child, and you Dyson. I'm thrilled beyond words that the two of you are here with me, too."

That night, as they were heading to bed, after kissing her grandda on the head, she remembered that she hadn't called the police as yet. She was making her a list of things to do tomorrow when she laid her head on the pillow. Christ, sleep was never too far behind in her being able to lie her head down.

Chapter 7

"Hello." Tabby was about as pissed off at her brother as she'd ever been. "Is anyone there?"

"Yes, I'm calling about the sale that you're having." She said it wasn't until the next morning. "I wanted to know —"

"Let me cut you off right there. No, I'm not going to go through the pallets and tell you exactly what we have. I'm not going to set aside the best of the lot for you to come by and look over. It's a sale on pallets. You'll be picking what you want from the stacked pallets. I can tell you that we have more root vegetables than fruit. Also, there will be no discounts on how many pallets that you take." The person, a woman, laughed. "I have a lot of work to be done, and I still have to answer calls like this. It said right on the paper not to call until after five."

"It is after five." She looked at the big clock on the wall and noticed that it was five-thirty. "I take it you've had people calling all day with those exact questions. I wasn't going to ask but to see if I could come by tonight and buy the entire lot from you."

"Sight unseen, and you'll take it all." She told her that she had a lot of people to feed. "I'm sure you think this might help, but you'd have to use this stuff within the next week. Some of it even less. I'm not going to give you a discount either. I just need it off my docks."

"Good. I can bet here in…she said in five minutes. More than likely less, but she has to find some hotspots before she can make it there." She asked her what she was talking about. "Is that going to work for you? I'll even sign something that says we came an hour later with the trucks—which are on their way to you now. She has cash, like you asked for, to pay you for all of them. Whatever the amount is."

"I don't understand. You're going to come back on me later, aren't you? Saying that I sold your store some shitty fruits and vegetables. Correct?" The woman, she'd not heard her name, said that she wasn't very trusting. "You have no idea how untrustful I am. I work with my brother and father, and they do shit like this and leave me to hold the bag. Christ, I need a drink and a vacation." She thought about what she'd said. "I'm sorry. I don't know why I just said that to you."

"It's fine. My colleague should be there now." A woman was walking towards her as the woman on the phone was talking. "Her name is Amy Walsh. We don't have a grocery store to use but I'm sure that it would sell. We have two shelters, not including a women's shelter in the county. There is a shelter too that serves two meals a day that we're going to donate the things to as well as there are a great many people in our town alone that would benefit greatly by having some fresh vegetables and fruit."

"I'm so sorry. I shouldn't have been so nasty to you." The woman told her that it was fine. It sounded like she was having a crappy day. "You have no idea. My brother, Earl, he's been running the business since our parents went on a cruise. He's good at it most of the time. We've worked together before. But this time, it's like he keeps getting these hair brained ideals that get me stuck with trying to sort it out. The too old produce? It's only one of the seven things that he's done to make me pissy with him. We're a fresh warehouse, and he bought fish. How the hell do I get rid of seven hundred pounds of salmon. Not to mention the cost of it." She sat down on the corner of her desk. "My name is Tabitha Reader. I didn't catch your name if you told me."

"Emma Walsh." She thought that she'd heard that name before and knew it when she began talking again. "We're trying to bring businesses into our little town and surrounding areas so that there will be jobs for everyone that wants them."

"I don't suppose you have about five hundred

acres for sale, do you? I need to enlarge my footprint, and that's not happening with where we are now." She asked her if she was serious. "I believe that I am. I wouldn't close this warehouse down. There are a lot of locals that take advantage of how fresh things can get to them. But since we do a lot of business in your area and surrounding states, having another, larger place would triple our business so that we don't have to turn away so many customers."

"It just so happens that we do have that much land that we can sell, actually, about twice that. There are a lot of farmers going out of business around here due to lack of help. I'm not saying that you'd have no one working for you. However, it would be a great place to have the kind of business that you have. It's just off a major highway and there are some new hotels going up surrounding the area that would accommodate the drivers when need be." Emma went on to tell her of the other perks there would be. "I can see this working out for both of us. I won't have to divide up the land for smaller places and there are enough lands around here that drivers could also benefit from some newer gas stations going in."

They didn't talk for long because she wanted to get Amy Walsh taken care of. When she showed her what she had in the way of crates of too-old things that her brother had purchased, she did indeed buy it all.

She said that within the next hour, they would have two refrigerator trucks there to take it back to Ohio. And the influx of cash getting it sold off made up for a couple of more of her brother's mistakes.

"Emma said that you have fish." She explained how she had salmon that would go bad if they didn't have a buyer within the next few days. "We'll take it. All of it. Name your price and we'll have the local pack help us with getting it into freezers around the county."

It occurred to her what a pack was. But in all the time that she'd been with Amy, she'd never once seen her on the phone. The two of them had some sort of link going on, and she was nervous about that. Tabby didn't know why she was nervous, but it was making her especially tense to know that these women were talking to one another, and she wasn't privy to the conversation that would be about her.

"You're all right." Nodding, she told Amy that she thought she would be. "No, I mean, you're not wrong in that we're talking about you, but we're thrilled with your help in this, and it was all good."

"You read my mind." She only grinned, and for some reason, that pissed her off. "I'd rather you didn't do that. What I have in my head is private."

"I understand, but I wanted to tell you that you're going to be all right when you go home tonight, too. He's gone." Tabby sat down and didn't know how to ask her if he really was. "Yes. He really is. You were smart to have the locks changed as soon as he was gone and that you took your money out of your bank and put it into another."

"He was robbing me. Selling things that belonged to me. Taking from my accounts and…I don't even want to know how you know this, but I'm grateful all the same." She could feel the tears filling her eyes as she looked at Amy. "Is he really gone? I'm not asking you if he'll be back, I'm sure that he'll try something, but he's not in my house any longer, correct?"

"Yes, I promise you that he's gone, and the police are there now to make sure he doesn't return before the locks are changed. I did that for you. I thought that once he got to the bank and found out that you changed things around, he'd go back and try to take something else. Perhaps do some serious damage to your home." Tabby couldn't help it. She burst into tears. "I have you. You're all right."

With the other woman's arms around her, she told her everything that had been going on over the last six months. It had been a nightmare when she woke up one morning, and he had moved into her house.

"I'd been out with him a couple of times. Levi had seemed like a decent person, he paid for the meals that we went to. I took him to a couple of functions that I was required to go to. We'd never had sex or anything. Not even a kiss at the door. He was like…I guess I thought of him as a friend more than anything. Then, about eight months ago, he started telling me that he needed money. I didn't give him any and was going to break off all contact with him. It must have pissed him off because a month later, no more than about six weeks, he moved into my home and was holding my daughter hostage. You have no idea what I had to do in order to get her out of the house and away from him." When she didn't say anything but continued to hold her, she finally had to tell someone what had happened. "I pushed my daughter down the stairs. She had on a helmet and I wrapped her up well so that she'd not break anything important like her neck."

"How old is she?" She told her that she was fourteen. She'd had her when she was sixteen. "I'm assuming that she was all right after you pushed her."

"Yes, a broken leg. It was her idea. She knew that if she could get away from him, then I could get away too. We'd planned it for a week and when he went out to get pizza, taking my car with him, the two of us did it. She was right. It got her out of the house for a few days, and now he's gone." Amy told her that she was proud of the two of them. "You don't think I'm a monster for making my daughter fall down the stairs and hurting her?"

"A monster? No, I don't think that at all. You were desperate. I'm assuming that you didn't involve your parents or brother in what was going on." She told her that she couldn't. They'd been so supportive when she'd gotten pregnant that she couldn't bring them in on something she'd done a second time. "They sound like a good family to have around. And I'm sure that they would have done anything to get you out of the situation, but I don't know, and it worked. As I said, I'm very proud of the two of you."

She felt stupid after telling a stranger what she'd done, but it also felt good. Her daughter, Mandy, was going to be released in a couple of days, and after that they were going to live in a hotel for a few days. Neither one of them wanted to stay in the house again. It had somehow been tainted by Levi. Besides, they were both looking forward to being pampered for a few days at a posh hotel.

They did very well today on getting the salmon and the crates sold off. When the trucks pulled into the lots, she was thrilled that one of them was a freezer truck. That way, the salmon would be able to last a bit longer. And it didn't hurt for it to be slightly frozen for a couple of days, what the trip would take back to their home place.

Tabby sat in her office after everyone else had

gone for the day and brought out the map of Ohio. With the exact coordinates, she was able to find where the land was that was for sale. It was just what she said it was, a bit of scrub that would need to be taken care of, but it was the highway that she was most interested in. It looked to be only a short four miles from where they would build their new warehouse. Printing out a copy of the area, she gathered up her things and made her way to the hospital. She needed to see Mandy in the worst sort of way.

There was a police officer outside her door when she got there, and it scared her to no end that Levi had gotten to her daughter. Rushing inside without asking the officer what she was doing there, it was Mandy who she could only think about.

"I called in a couple of favors." Pausing outside the room before rushing in, she tried to figure out who was speaking to her and how they were doing it. "It's Amy. I wanted to help you keep Mandy safe. And the favor was something that I could do for you. There will be police there until you're released. To speak back, all you need to do is think about what you want to say to me. Hopefully, it will be nicer than you were thinking of your brother." Tabby laughed a little.

"I never thought of that. He might well have gotten her while I was changing the locks." Amy told her that he'd been arrested for trespassing, but he was going to be able to get out soon. He also made a scene at the bank. "Good. If they can keep him there for a few days, then we can get into a hotel." Amy told her to go and enjoy her daughter.

"Hey, mom." She kissed Mandy on her forehead and handed her the things that she'd brought her from the store. "I might get to go home in a couple of days."

Every time she looked at her, she ached for what she'd done to her only child. She'd actually tossed her down the stairs like she was nothing. Crying with Mandy holding her, she told her again and again how sorry she was. Mandy, of course, thought that she did exactly what was needed and now they were free. They weren't free, and she was sure that Mandy knew it, but for now, they were able to visit without Levi intruding on their time together. Mandy asked her how work was going.

She told her how she'd been able to get the stuff sold that her uncle Tommy had bought as well as she was one day ahead of the shipments going out tomorrow. Getting permission from the shop owners on the plan for them to get their items one day early had made three companies happy.

"Tommy wasn't happy that I'd sold it all at once, but he'll get over it. I think he was just mad because he had to send out notices that the sale wasn't going to happen. Also, the seafood is gone, too. Dad called about the time I was telling Tommy to not do that again and he agreed with me. Telling Tommy to not do anything like that unless we had a buyer lined up. I don't know but I think that the Walsh family will buy anything that we can get to them." Mandy snapped her fingers, telling her what someone named Walsh had sent to her. "My goodness, child. This is nice. A tablet and things for you to read. That's pretty special for a stranger to give to you."

"I thought so too, but I didn't get to see anyone when it was brought. The hospital staff brought it up here." She showed her the beautiful vase of flowers, too. "It was like she knew that my favorite flowers were daisies and roses." Tabby was sure that she did know that and a great deal more about the two of them than was necessary for business acquaintances.

After visiting with Mandy, Tabby went by her parent's home to bring in the mail. Also, she watered her dad's plants and made sure that there were no leaks anywhere as well as checking the thermostat to make sure the furnace was still working. Just as she was about to leave, a strange car pulled into the driveway. She stayed hidden within the shadows to see who it was.

When someone touched her mind, she nearly screamed. Tabby had never been so happy with the person who told her that it was Amy and that she had her.

"Do you see the little person on the table where you are? He said to tell you that you don't have to have him touch you, but he's there to help you." She looked at the table and didn't see anything at first. "He's about four inches tall and is blue. His name is Barber. They pick their own names, so you'd not believe the names that they come up with. One was called Marlon Brando. Like it was all one word. Then—"

"You're babbling or giving me time to come to grips with my fear." She told her that it was both. "All right. I'm better." Then she saw the little man. "I see Barber. Am I dead already?"

"No. Goodness no. He's there to help you. Let him land on your palm." She asked Amy if she was sure. "Yes. Once he's there, no one will see either of you. The man is coming into the house soon. I've called the police and said that you were the caller. I want you to stand right where you are so that Barber can keep you safe."

The front door exploded open and the alarm that was on the whole house began to scream loudly throughout the house. She thought for sure that the man was going to ignore the sounds but almost as soon as he stepped into the dining room where she was, he turned and left. Still, neither she nor her new best friend Barber moved until the police pulled into the driveway.

~*~

Emma was ready to go home and not hire anyone when the two women came and had a seat where she was conducting interviews. Not only did they have a copy of their license, but they also brought her a copy of their certificate from the training center where they got their permission — or whatever it was called to drive the big rigs. They were tandem drivers, they told her.

"My name is Danielle, and this is my sister Shelby Pennebaker. We've been driving for the last five years and have done well." She thought that the two of them could have been models; they were so beautiful. But it seemed to her, too, that they had no desire to be anything but drivers. "My grandda was a driver, my parents were tandem drivers until we were born, then it was just him. After our mom passed away, he'd take us on the road, and we learned a great deal from him."

"Do you own your own rig?" That was something that she needed to know, and when they said that they did, with a refrigerant hook-up, she wanted to hire them on the spot. But she had a guideline, and she was going to follow it. "How much traveling did you want to do? Or do you just want local?"

"We don't have a home, so it doesn't matter where you send us. That's the reason that we have our own rig so that we've had it built for us." Danielle looked at her sister as they continued. "We don't need to work. We've both been made wealthy by insurance from when our family was alive, and now we find moving around together is all we need."

"I would think that you'd not like being together like that." She laughed when they did. "Do you fight a great deal? That's just me asking. I've no brothers or sisters to compare my life with except for a step-sister who is a great deal older than I am."

"We grew up practically in the back of a rig. We were all we had, and it was considered wrong to have your kids with you when driving. So, we learned very quickly to get along no matter what, and we do the same now. Not that we don't have our differences, but we don't have fights like a lot of drivers with their tandem drivers have."

She could see that they were close, and for some reason, she trusted that they would do a good job for them when they were overseeing the warehouse products that they were planning on getting. The fruits and vegetables that they got earlier in the week had given them a boost like they'd not thought of, and they were going to try and do the same again and again.

After the two of them left, Emma only had three more people to interview. She didn't want to but she had said that she'd knock these interviews out of the way so that they could get started on a few other projects that they had going on. She'd been by the pack yesterday and was happy that they'd been able to use nearly everything that had been purchased from Tabby. And they'd been able to make forty-four pies and put them into the freezer for when they needed them. It had worked out beautifully for a great many people.

When she got home, she was happy to see that Dyson was there. Even though he was on his office phone, she did go in and kiss him in greeting. Her grandda was in the kitchen having a light lunch with the cook and having a great time.

"I was just telling Beth here that I'd like to have some of that salmon she has in the freezer. That's my favorite dish, as you well know." She said that she did know that and wouldn't mind some at all. "I tried to explain to her how you cook it, but I messed it all up. If you could tell her, I'd be thrilled beyond anything about it. It's about the best that I've ever eaten."

After telling Beth how it was cooked, her grandda wandered off to go in the backyard. He loved spending time there, and with Darling still behind bars with her daughter, it was easier for him to get around town, too. Her grandda would be one hundred years old in a couple of months, and he was getting around better than he had in the last five years. She loved this magic for him so very much.

After dinner, all of them enjoying the fresh salmon, they decided that the weather was just perfect for them to go into town and get some dessert. Grandda and Dyson loved banana splits and she had herself a malt. That was what she loved more than just plain ice cream in a bowl. However, she didn't care for shakes. The tastes weren't the same.

"I have me a little job. That little girl, Amy hired me to wander around town when the weather is good and listen to what people are needing. She sure did, with the rest of you fellers, make a good dent in people going hungry this year. Those vegetables surely did fill a lot of bellies and freezers this year. And you getting anyone that could afford it a freezer at cost sure has made them people love what's going on in their town." Emma said that she'd noticed too that a great many more people are volunteering at the pack house to help separate out of the foods. "Yeah, I saw that too. And letting people come and get what they wanted was good to do. I know that the women's shelter was the happiest of the groups that I've ever seen."

They were planning a clothing drive in the next couple of weeks. It wasn't just for the children of the town so much as to have a shop set up where people could come and get what they needed—adults to children. The Walsh family had purchased two washer and dryer sets so that they could clean up everything that was brought in. She was having the time of her life helping with so many projects around town and into the county.

"Did Amy tell you about the near robbery of Tabby's parents' home? It was a couple of nights ago. The robber had noticed that the family car wasn't moving, and he decided that when Tabby was there, he'd go in and get her to open the safe if there was any. She was lucky that Amy had a connection with her or there is no telling what might have happened." Dyson said that she had a faerie now that watched over her and her daughter, who is home from the hospital now. They're staying in one of the larger hotel chains until they sell their home. I'm not sure what that's about, but she might be moving this way."

"That's great. Maybe she's the mate of one of the other brothers." Dyson said he was joking, but Emma had been thinking the same thing. Then there was the Pennebaker women. They were both single and moving to this area as well. She told them about the two of them. "Twins, huh? Well, that would be awesome. To have all these pretty women around for the others... not that it would matter to them, I don't think. Believe it or not, I think that Edgar is really looking forward to having a mate. He isn't even looking for himself a house yet so that they can pick it out together."

"I don't think that Sidney is looking for a mate. I believe that he feels like he's going to be alone for the rest of his life. He is a great man, and I have no idea why he'd think that, but that's what he's been saying for a few weeks now. He'll just be the best uncle to all the kids we have." All three of them got a kick out of that. Of the six boys, as they were called, Sidney was the biggest flirt and had the most fun with women all the time. "When he gets his mate I think he's going to be hit hard with the love that they create. He's going to be a good father, too, to whoever comes along."

"I agree. That boy, he's a good one. Any woman and some men would consider themselves lucky to have such a person in their corner." Grandda saw a friend of his coming out of the store and left them there. He really was having a grand time doing his little job for the community.

Hand in hand, Dyson walked home with her. She told him about the interviews that she'd done, and he asked her questions about the twins. They were looking for people with their own rigs so they'd not have to put out that kind of money.

However they were going to have trailers to have around so that they could pick things up quickly and have them delivered where they needed to be. Purchasing ten large freezers for the foundation had helped a great deal, and they were hoping to keep them filled up for anything that came along. Amy was helping with that and Layla was in charge of where things were to be taken to.

So far, the only room they had that much space in was the pack house. Fowler was making sure that they were being well compensated for their help and that of the storage as well. They even shared the food that they got with them for their time. They had been contacted by two other food and storage warehouses to get leftovers, and Emma thought that it was wonderful. No more wasted food like they had before.

"It broke my heart to know that they would just toss the food out when it got to be too old to sell. Tabby told me that most of the time, the stuff is good-looking, too. It's just that when you calculated the time it took to have it loaded on a truck and then delivered to the store, it was too late for them to get it out on the floor for a very long time." Dyson said he'd not thought of that, the store turnover. "She said that there are a lot of things that have to be calculated into selling fruit especially. If it's too ripe when it's loaded on the truck the first time, it might well be rotten when it gets to them even."

"Something to think about the next time we're in a store. You know, how long it's been on a truck from first being picked." He shook his head. "Isn't it funny how you never thought of these kinds of things before, but now that you know about it, it's all you can think about."

"I know." They were nearly home when grandda called. He was going to be playing chess with some buddies of his and would be home late. He also told them that someone was going to be bringing him home. She loved that old man and was happy to see him out and about with springs in his steps.

Chapter 8

"May I help you?" Emma smiled at the door, knowing that someone was looking at her through the little hole in it. "I'm not going to open the door until you tell me who you are."

"Emma Walsh. We spoke the other day when I interviewed the two of you. I don't know if you're going to remember me or not." She heard the door unlock then the door opened. "I'm sorry if I'm too late. I didn't think of the time when I came here."

"It's fine. We were just enjoying a nice comfy bed for a change. We don't normally take a hotel room when we have work to do, but we were told that you guys were going to let us know tonight if we got the job or not. To be honest with you, I'm thinking that with you coming here, it's a nice way of letting us down. But hey, we weren't looking for a job when we did this, so—"

"You have the job." The squeal that Danielle let out was ear-bursting. The two sisters hugged and jumped on the bed like they were in preschool or something. "I'm glad I came by to tell you rather than you having to hear about it on the phone. This was wonderful."

They both hugged her as well and encouraged her to jump on the bed as well. It was fun and enjoyable to be around this much excitement about a job. It was Shelby who spoke first.

"We were getting sick of the hit-and-miss of a job. More and more people are becoming drivers, and it's getting hard to find a job. We're both so thrilled to be able to work for a company. You have no idea." After they settled down, she handed them their contracts as well as some of the perks that they were going to be getting. "I really appreciate being able to haul both ways. It costs so much to have to come back from a job empty."

"You'll also be happy to know that we're going to be helping out the warehouse that's in Tennessee. She's going to be putting another plant up here to reach the New England states. It'll be a lot of driving at first, but we'll settle that down once things are in place here." They both looked over the contract. "There is something else that you need to be aware of. The Walsh family aren't human."

"Yeah, we figured that out on our own. Both of us are wolf shifters, so it matters little to us that you're not." Danielle smiled at her. "We have a bit of magic of our own, so if you were going to tell us that we got some from this job, that would be all right with us if we didn't mingle with our stuff."

"I'm afraid that's too late." She put out her hand, and two of the faeries that she'd brought with her landed on her hand. "This is Bobin and Robin. They get to pick their names when they're assigned to a person. They'll be with you at all times when you're driving. It's not to spy on you but to keep you safe. I don't know how much trouble you've had at being women drivers but these guys will help you out of any situation that you might find yourself in."

The two women looked at each other. She could tell they were talking to one another but what they were saying, she didn't have a clue. When they finally looked at her, she had a feeling that they did have a problem with other drivers when out.

"About two months ago now we were at a truck stop when Shelby was jumped. Lucky for her, she was a wolf, or she might not have been able to get away. Since then, we've had two more attacks on us, and it's been scary. We have never had that kind of issue before. But like we said, there are more and more drivers out, and some of them aren't as nice as the company they work for thinks they are." She asked if they had reported them. "You have a code around truckers. You simply get back to them in a more personal way. Getting them fired only makes it worse. We took care of all three of the attackers, and we're better off for it."

She didn't want to know and was glad that they didn't tell her. It made her realize that she needed to get with the local pack and see what sort of things she might be missing by hiring shifter wolves. Or any shifter, for that matter. Did they have different rules than each other when it came to protecting themselves? Was it all right to take justice into their own hands? She didn't know but thought that it might be best if she found out.

When she was ready to leave the two women, she made her way home. Dyson was working late at the house, and when she entered, his office lights were still on. Grandda, she was sure, had gone to bed a while ago. He was an early riser and went to bed early as well.

"How did it go?" She told Dyson that it had gone well. That they were excited to have the faeries as well. "Good. I'm assuming that they'll be ready to start in the next couple of days. Layla told me that she has three more places where we can pick up day-old things. Also, the local grocery store is going to allow us to have all their fruit that is beyond selling. So long as we don't sell it."

"I wouldn't do that. We have too many people that are in need of a boost up and selling them things that we get for them would just be wrong on so many levels. How did your meeting go with your grandma?" He told her that it went very well and that she was on board with letting the faeries help with a couple of projects that they had going on. "Good. Getting them to help with the building of the new offices for the school and the grade school upgrades will help a great many people."

"Before I forget. Grandma invited us to have dinner with her tomorrow night. I told her that I'd ask you but didn't foresee any trouble with that. I'm glad that we share a calendar, Emma. You've no idea how much that's saved me over the last two days." She told him that it had her as well. "Also, something else. There are some inspectors coming to the warehouse that we're using for food distribution. I don't think that they'll ding us for much, if anything at all. Again the faeries are making sure that the place is in tip-top shape every hour so that nothing is going to be harmful for the people that are getting things from it."

"It helps too that there are no mice within a hundred miles of the place." Dyson laughed and said that did help, yes. "I need to get with the pack about some things that came up. Nothing that would involve us, but I need to understand a few things about shifters of their kind. I'm going to do the same for any shifter that we hire, but I just found out that the Pennebaker women are wolves."

"I knew that. I'll have to show you how to figure out the differences between humans and shifters soon so that you're not blindsided." She said that she'd like that. "All right. Anything else before we go to bed? I'm exhausted and could probably sleep for a month without stirring. It's been a very long few days, and I'm ready for some downtime."

"I am as well. We don't have anything in the morning, so how about we turn off our phones and wake up when we want to instead of when the alarm goes off?" He thought that was an excellent idea. "Good. You should tell your family too. Just so they don't contact you for anything other than an emergency. All right?"

Emma was actually excited to be going to bed and not having to be a slave to the alarm going off on her phone. As she was getting ready for bed, simply stripping down to nothing but her bare skin, all she could think about was how warm she wanted to be and to sleep the sleep of the dead. Her body ached to be rested. It was nearly noon when the two of them woke up. It was back to work but she felt so much better for it.

~*~

Dyson was getting his desk cleaned off when Emma joined him in his office. Grandda had left, telling him that he had a few things to look into before dinner.

Whatever it was, the older man was having fun with his new 'job,' and Dyson couldn't have been happier for him.

"We have the house to ourselves." He asked where the cook had gone. "Something about a big sale on kitchenware. I hope you don't mind but I gave her one of the credit cards you gave me and told her that if she had any trouble to call. She was about as excited as I've ever seen her. What is kitchenware anyway?"

He laughed. "I don't know, honestly. I'd say pots and pans, but I have a feeling it's a bit more than that. Dishes perhaps? I don't know either. But if she'll cook us better dinners because of it, then I'll be one fat dragon but sated when it comes to food." He could tell that she had something on her mind and waited. Talking nonsense while he waited on her. "The ground has been broken for the new warehouse that Tabby is going to be using. The faeries will go in at night and work on it so that it gets done faster. Fowler said a great many people showed up asking Tabby about the job situation." She nodded. When she looked at him, she smiled.

"Instead of babbling, why don't you come here, strip me out of my clothing, and make love to me?" His cock jerked in his pants. All day, he thought of ways he wanted to take his new love and that was when he realized that he had fallen in love with her. "I have this new panties and bra set on that I got yesterday while I was out with the other women. And some other pretties that I want to tease you with."

"Show me." He smiled when she started to unbutton her blouse. Then she spread her legs wide enough that he could see a hint of yellow silk between her legs. "I love silk. Especially when it's on you." He inhaled deeply. "I love the way you smell when you're ready for me to make love to you. Also, you might want to know that you're in heat, or whatever it's called by dragon lore. We could create a child should you wish." She nodded, her eyes darkening while she sat on his desk in front of him.

The blouse was opened by two of the tiniest buttons that he'd ever seen. He could see little of the treats beneath it. When she sat up a little, using his shoulders as leverage, she pulled the skirt she had on off and let it drop to the floor. Her legs opened for him, and he could see that she was wet, that she'd stained the silky material with her juices. That was what he could smell on her. Heat and pure sex.

When she slid the blouse down her shoulders, she held it over her breasts. He wanted to see her, all of her, and reached down to stroke his cock through his pants. She moaned when he scooted down in his seat and opened his fly. His cock sprang forward like it knew just where it was going to be. Deeply inside of the woman that he loved.

"I'd like to suck on your cock." He nodded, not sure he was able to speak around his sudden need to feel her doing just that. "Would you like that? To come down my throat?"

"Yes. Come here." She moved then, letting the blouse go, and he could see her dark nipples under the sheer material of her bra. "Take it off for me. Let me see all of you."

When she reached behind her to unhook her bra, Dyson pulled his pants down to his knees and wrapped his hand around his cock. He was painfully hard now; precum was dripped from the tip in a long stream, and he used it to fist himself. But when she took her bra off and dropped it to the floor with the rest of her clothing, he nearly jerked his dick off when she cupped her breast and licked at the tip of her full breast.

"Christ, do that again." She did it to both her nipples, leaving them wet with her tongue. When she moved toward him, wearing only a pair of panties and her warm flesh, he wanted to beg her to let him eat her, but she was at his knees before he could make his tongue move to form words. When her hands moved to take his cock, he held onto the arms of the chair as she licked him from root to tip. When it broke off in his hand, he laughed a little out of pure desperation. And need.

Starting at the root of his cock, following the thick vein up to the tip, she lapped at his cock, taking all his cum into her mouth. When she leaned back on her knees, he wanted to jerk her up from the floor and slam into her. Christ, his head was buzzing just thinking about what she was doing to him.

"You taste as good as you smell." Dyson nodded not caring what she was saying so long as she finished him. When she took his crown in her mouth and sucked, he nearly came up out of the chair. "Don't touch me, Dyson. I want to explore you without you rushing me."

"I want to come in your mouth. On your body." Emma nodded at him and smiled. Then she leaned over him and swallowed him down past the tightness of her throat. "Holy Christ, love, I'm there."

He came. He might have thought that he could hold off, perhaps make it last longer but as soon as she tightened those lovely muscles at the back of her throat around him, Dyson knew it was too much. Curling his hand at the back of her head, he filled her. His cock emptied deep into her and filled again as she fucked him with her mouth.

Christ, he'd never been one to take his enjoyment before a woman, but he had a feeling that it was going to be hard for him not to with her. When he came a second time, his balls tight against his body, he pulled her up off the floor and jerked her down over his cock. The look on her face, the look of pure joy, had him taking them both to the floor and him plowing her hard.

"I want to come." He told her he wanted her to as well. "Please, fill me, Dyson. I want to feel you come inside of my pussy. Create a child with me so that we can continue our line."

He held her body to his. Fucked her harder than he had any woman before her and knew that she'd be sore in the morning. But the harder he took her, the more he fucked her, the more she begged him for. And when she dug her nails into his back, feeling the blood as it moved down his back, Dyson felt her body tighten around his, and she screamed out her release.

He watched her face as she came. Dyson knew for as long as he lived, the vision of her coming, her entire being releasing for him would be something that he'd never forget. Something that would keep him warm on nights when she was sleeping beside him. As he threw back his head, his own body letting go, his dragon roared inside of him. Complete. He was, and they were complete with this woman.

Dropping down on her, his body spent, he rolled to his back, holding her over him. His heart was aching it had pounded so hard. His breath was hot, his dragon letting him know that he was pleased as well. As he lay there, holding onto the woman who had come to mean more to him in the last month than any had in all his life, Dyson fell as deeply in love with his other half as he knew he was supposed to.

Waking up, he found himself on the floor alone. Hearing voices down the hall, he was just too spent to get up hurriedly and get dressed. Willing himself to be clothed, he lay there for a few minutes longer, realizing that the voices weren't getting any closer than they were when he woke. He did, however, sit up and lean against his desk.

"Are you all right?" He laughed, his body hurting just a little when Emma asked him. He told her that he didn't think he was ever going to be all right again. "Good, at least we have that in common. I'd love to do that again but I think we have to be more careful of being caught. I'd just gotten up when Grandda came home. I shut the door to the office and told him that you were busy with reports. We're in the kitchen now if you want to join us. If you can, that is."

"Making fun of a man when he's down isn't nice, you know?" He stood up, holding onto the desk until he could get his feet under him. He looked at his chair. "I'm afraid I'm going to need a new chair. This one suffered badly." She laughed, and it did his heart good to hear it. "All right. I'm on my way, but I could use a large glass of something wet and cold. I think I hurt myself when I came."

"All I can think about is that we might well have created a child for us. I love you so much, Dyson. I never knew in all my life that something like love, a little four-letter word, could feel so good when you have it for someone, and they have it for you as well." He was humbled by her words. "Come to the kitchen with me. We're having subs that my grandda requested. We're just waiting for you to come join us."

Dyson only just realized that he was starving. He wanted subs, fries, a milkshake, a pie—not a slice but an entire pie for his meal. Going into the kitchen, he was glad to see that someone had predicted that he was hungry and had two subs on a plate for him. There were also Saratoga fries too. Christ, if he kept burning energy with Emma, he was going to need to eat like this at least a few times a week.

After dinner, he made his way back to the office. He had things that he needed to look into, and Grandda wanted to go. Checking on the houses that were being built for the homeless was coming along much faster than he realized. Not only were three of them about finished up, but the things for the kitchen had been stabilized so that they couldn't be taken out but with magic. No one would get by with stealing things from the new houses, and he was going to make sure of it.

There were sleeping bags, too, until the mattresses and beds came in. Just as they were returning home, having picked up a gallon of ice cream from the grocery store, he saw Darling and David. He told Grandda.

"I seen them. Looking pretty down on their luck, wouldn't you say?" He had to agree with him. "Oh well, no hope for it, they saw me. Don't leave me, young man. I need to have you around so that I can hold me a great grandbaby someday."

"Sooner than you expect, old man." He just looked at him and Dyson nodded when he told him that they were expecting. It would be about five months for the hatchling to be born then about another six months for it to hatch.

He could see that he wanted answers and Dyson told him that they had to take care of this right now. Looking back at his daughter, there was a smile on the elderly man's face that looked as if it could light up the world. And all it took for him to look like that was knowing that Emma was going to have a child.

"I need some cash." Grandda said he was glad to see her, too, and he was having a wonderful day. "Like we care what sort of day you're having. I need enough money to hire me an attorney that will get me out of this shit. Also, I'm moving into the house with you. You need a keeper, and I'm going to be keeping your shit from getting away from me."

"I don't even know why you'd care where my poop was coming from or why you'd want it. But you're not moving in with us, and I'm not going to give you any money. I'm in a really good mood, Darling, and you're not going to be taking that away from me either." Dyson watched as David seemed to be trying to get between him and the other man. Moving in a way that blocked him, David started to fall forward just as he pulled Grandda back.

"What do you think you're doing, knocking me around? I'll have your ass for this, see that I don't." Dyson looked up at the cameras that were all along the street. The one pointed at him, and the others had only been up for a few days. "I don't care what that says about what happened. We need money, and you're going to give it to us before I tell everyone what a monster you are."

"If you mean a dragon, everyone already knows that. And I'm not a monster but a very wealthy man who just so happens to be able to change into a great dragon. Would you like to see him? I can spread out for you right now if that's what you want." He let just enough of his dragon go to prove to David and Darling that he wasn't joking. "It's up to you but I've already had a nice dinner but would chew you two up just to have you gotten rid of."

"That's just disgusting. There is no way that

you're going to eat us. We're humans, and that would be against the law." He told Darling that he thought there were a great many people who would be thrilled if she and her husband were gone. "You think that? Well, you'd be wrong. People adore us." Dyson stopped the next person who came out of the shop they were near.

"Hey? Do you know this couple?" The woman glared at David and looked at him, telling him there wasn't a person in town who didn't know about the Gregory couple. "She said that people adore her and him. Is that how you feel—"

He never got to finish. The woman was laughing so hard that she had to hold onto the wall to keep herself upright. And every time she looked at the other couple, she laughed all the harder. In just a few minutes, he'd asked four other people, and they had the same reaction. Like having to adore them was the funniest thing that they'd ever heard in their lives.

Dyson was just ready to ask another person when Darling slapped him. It wasn't hard enough to hurt him. He was a shifter, after all, as well as a dragon. But she did draw blood, and that pissed him off. Just a little. He gave himself a talk about how he was going to be a dad soon, and he didn't want to be in jail for killing Darling when it was born. Besides, he was reasonably sure that Emma would strangle him if he were to end up there.

Letting enough of his dragon go, he was able to get to his claws on his hand before Grandda put his hand over it. Turning to look at him, his eyes seeing him in blues and reds instead of the human that he was, he shook his head.

"She's not worth it, Dyson. Not at all. If you want to press charges for her hitting you, I can back you up, but don't kill her. I have a feeling that Emma would be surely angry at you." He pulled his dragon back and felt the pain of something searing through his body.

She'd shot him. It didn't hurt that bad; he was protected from such things, but when he fell back, taking her with him and the gun, it went off a second time, and he didn't know where that ended up. Lying still on the sidewalk, he tried to reason with his dragon in that killing her now would be wrong.

He still hadn't moved when the police arrived. David was on the ground as well, but he couldn't see what he was doing. If he was honest with himself, he was hurting a bit more than he thought from a simple gun. It wasn't until his brother showed up and Melbourne told him that he'd been shot in the chest. Too near his heart for him to just get up and walk around.

"Play it, young man." He looked at Grandda.

The man seemed to be swaying around. "You're all right, Dyson, but play this part well."

It wasn't until Darling was pulled off of him that he realized that she was dead. The shot through her head told him that, as a human, she wouldn't recover from this. As he was being told to be still, he got a look at David. He, too, had been shot.

"How are you, Dyson?" He said that he was hurting now. "Well, I hate to sound like a fool, but I'm glad that you're hurting. I surely am." He looked at the officer that was near him.

"I don't know what happened. We were talking, and then I heard something pop. Did she shoot me?" The officer told him that she had shot him and he'd appreciate it if he didn't die too. "I didn't shoot her, sir. I swear. She came at me after hitting me."

"We know that. Grandda here. He's been telling us what happened. How that shot was able to go through her into her husband is one for the books. We know that she pulled the trigger, too. The gun is tight in her hands." He asked him again how he was feeling. "I have to talk to your wife and I don't want to have to give her any bad news. She's a mite scary when she's upset, you know."

"I've never been shot before." He had been, but he didn't think anyone would believe him if he told them that it had been wartime and that he'd been on the right side of the law. "Is David really dead, too?"

Before he could answer him, he heard screaming and someone cursing at him. He didn't move, not even when he felt Emma coming to him. As soon as she touched him, he felt better, not great, but better. The screaming person was Poppy, the daughter of the dead couple.

"She killed them. Just like I knew that she would. She killed them dead, and I want to sue her for her money." The officer, he couldn't for the life of him remember his name, said that it was her mother who had killed them both. "I won't believe it. My mother was a saint, and she'd—"

"Oh, do grow up. Neither you nor your parents were all that nice. And calling her a saint should be considered a deadly sin." The first woman he'd asked laughed a little. "You get yourself out of here before we tar and feather you. Saintly mother indeed. She was the devil herself if you were to ask anyone in this town. And you've been worrying that grandda of yours nearly to death since you were old enough to know what money was. Get going before I kick your ass. Damned girl. You're just lucky that no body asked me about you. You're worse than the two of them together. Get."

Poppy left, but she wasn't far when she turned back to the crowd that had gathered. With Emma holding his hand and Grandda close enough, he felt something close over him and was shocked to see Poppy pulling out a gun as well. Before she could get off a single shot, she was shot by the officer who was near him. And just like that, the entire Gregory family was gone.

The bodies were still lying on the sidewalk when he was taken away in the ambulance. He was glad that the officer was going to bring Emma and Grandda with him. He wanted them out of the way of the press when they showed up. It was a small town, but word would spread quickly, and it would be no time for some of the larger news organizations to get a hold of this. Three dead and one injured dragon would make great headlines, he thought with a little laugh.

Before You Go...

HELP AN AUTHOR

write a review

THANK YOU!

Share your voice and help guide other readers to these wonderful books. Even if it's only a line or two, your reviews help readers discover the author's books so they can continue creating stories that you'll love. Log in to your favorite retailer and leave a review. Thank you.

AWARD WINNING, BESTSELLING AUTHOR

Kathi Barton, a winner of the Pinnacle Book Achievement Award and a best-selling author on Amazon and All Romance books, lives in Nashport, Ohio, with her husband, Paul. When not creating new worlds and romance, Kathi and her husband enjoy camping and going to auctions. She can also be seen at county fairs with her husband, an artist and potter.

Her muse, a cross between Jimmy Stewart and Hugh Jackman, brings her stories to life for her readers in a way that has them coming back time and again for more. Her favorite genre is paranormal romance, with a great deal of spice. You can visit Kathi online and drop her an email if you'd like. She loves hearing from her fans. aaronskiss@gmail.com.

Follow Kathi on her blog: http://kathisbartonauthor.blogspot.com/